THE
WOMEN
IN THE
MIRROR

The Iowa
School of Letters
Award for Short Fiction

THE
WOMEN
IN THE
MIRROR

Pat Carr

University of Iowa Press
Iowa City, 1977

University of Iowa Press, Iowa City 52242

The previously published stories in this collection appear by permission:

"Progress Report—Candelaria Project," *Southern Review* 8 (Autumn 1969).

"Bullfight,"*Cairn* 10 (Autumn/Spring 1973-74).

"The Party," *Southern Review* 9 (Winter 1973). Reprinted in *The Best American Short Stories of 1974* (Houghton-Mifflin, 1975).

"Miss Amelia's," *Southern Review* 11 (Autumn 1975).

"Exiles," *Yale Review* 66 (Winter 1977).

Library of Congress Cataloging in Publication Data

Carr, Pat M   1932-
   The women in the mirror.

   (The Iowa School of Letters award for short fiction)
   CONTENTS: The party.—Miss Amelia's.—Sunday morning. [etc.]
   I. Title.   II. Series.
PZ4. C3123Wo [PS3553.A7633] 813'.5'4   77-24965
ISBN 0-87745-081-1
ISBN 0-87745-082-X pbk.

For Duane Carr

Prize money for the award is provided by a grant from the Iowa Arts Council.

CONTENTS

THE PARTY

I STEADIED THE present on my lap and took a deep breath that stopped at my tight damp skirt band. The street-car wheels clicked, clicked against the rails. I resisted the impulse to push back wet strands of hair at my temples and mash what little curl was left.

I didn't want to be on the hot trolley and I didn't want to go.

I pushed my glasses back up my greasy nose and wiped under the rims, carefully, not touching the glass with my knuckles. I had wanted so much more to stay in the porch swing with my book. John had just started telling his story; he was still with Beau and Digby, and we had all been together beneath sun spots of heat and sand, hearing the curses of the Legionnaires, smelling hot leather and camel fuzz. And then I had to splash tepid water over my face, change from my shorts and wrap the hasty present my mother had bought at the dime store that morning. Matching fingernail polish and lipstick whose perfume made me slightly nauseated, but that Jan would probably like all right. I guessed she would, anyway, but I didn't much care. I begrudged the time I was having to lose. Over forty minutes each way on the trolley, and I would have to stay at least until 4:30 before I could break away politely. They usually played some kind of games until about 3:30 or so before they let you eat and escape.

I looked at the fat bland face of the watch hanging in its leather sheath beside the conductor: 2:20. I'd be a little late as it was and that would mean even more minutes lost at the end of the party; my mother said you should always stay at least two hours for politeness' sake. And I had the other two Beau books waiting in their faded blue covers when I finished this one. My whole Saturday afternoon wasted.

The click of the metal wheels chipped away at my world of sand and dry hot fortresses until the desert sun fell into pieces and then dissolved. I scooted the damp package higher up on my lap. I could feel drops of sweat collecting under my bare knees.

We were passing the cemetery. The gawky stone angels dotted the tombs and oozed green slime. They all had the same faces, the same stone cataracts for eyes. Guardian angels, stiffened and blind.

I settled back against the wooden seat, feeling the wet patch of blouse on my skin as we swayed along. It would be another ten minutes on the trolley and then an eight block walk. My whole Saturday wasted.

When I climbed down from the awkward trolley steps, I realized the afternoon was even hotter than when I had started from home. The drops behind my knees gathered into rivulets that crawled with itching slowness down to the tops of my anklets. Hot branches hung like lank hair over the street, lifting and drooping with a faint hot breeze almost as if they were panting.

Half a block away I saw the house with its tight cluster of balloons tacked to the front door and its pink ribbon trailing from the brass knocker. Up close, I wasn't quite sure how to knock around the pink satin ribbon, so I finally used my knuckles and left damp imprints on the white door.

The door popped open immediately and a lady I guessed must be Jan's mother stood there beaming greedily at me.

"Here's your first guest," she half turned back and called happily without taking her eyes off me. "Do come in," she added to me and tried to open the door wider except that it was already open about as far as it could go. She reached out to take my arm, but when she saw me looking at her a little dumbfounded she didn't touch me and just motioned me in with her hand. I saw Jan behind her.

"Hi," I said, blinking a little with the shadow of the room as the door closed out the bright streak of balloons. I held out the little package with its moist wrapping paper.

"Hi," she said and took the package.

"Aren't you going to introduce your little friend to me, Jan?" her mother said brightly, birdlike, from beside me.

I winced and glanced at her as Jan mumbled my name and held the present in her hands, not seeming to know what to do with it. Although not as fat as Jan, her mother had the same tight curly hair and the same plump cheeks. She said something else bright and pecking while I was looking at her that I didn't hear and then she put a hand on each of our shoulders and pushed us slightly ahead of her into the next room.

"We decided to stack all the presents on the buffet, and yours can be the first," I could hear her beam from behind us.

The room was a dining room, but it was so covered with

pink crepe paper I couldn't tell at first. Pink twisted streamers bulged low from the overhead light and swung to the molding of every wall. The tablecloth was scalloped with pink crepe paper held on by Scotch tape, and the buffet where Jan's mother put my present was skirted with more taped pink paper. A massive pink frosted cake with a circle of twelve pink candles in flower holders sat in the center of the table, and the whole rest of the table top was jammed with pink paper plates holding a pink snapper each and a pink nut cup stuffed with cashew nuts. Enough for the whole class I guessed.

"We thought we'd just stand up for the cake and ice cream," her mother's voice smiled around me. I knew we would have pink ice cream with the cake. "We just don't have thirty-three chairs in the house," she almost giggled.

I didn't know what to say and Jan didn't say anything, so her voice added, "Why don't you show your little friend your new room, Jan? I'll be down here to catch the door as the rest of your guests arrive."

Jan made a kind of shrugging nod and led the way out the other side of the room, up some stairs that smelled of newly rubbed polish to a converted attic room.

Everything in the room was yellow. Bedspread, curtains, walls, lampshade on the desk. It was a bit like having been swallowed by a butterfly, but it wasn't as bad as the pink downstairs.

"It's new," Jan said offhandedly. "Daddy finished the walls and my mother made the bedspread and curtains." She glanced around casually, but I caught the glint of pride before she covered it up.

"It's nice," I said. "I like yellow."

"It's so sunny." I could almost hear her mother saying it.

I nodded and grappled for something else to talk about. "What's that?" I pointed to a cloth-covered scrap book. The cover was a tiny red and white check, and I somehow knew Jan had chosen that herself.

"Just some sketches." But she couldn't cover up the pride this time.

"Can I see them?" I said too heartily, but she didn't notice as she put the book tenderly on the bed.

I started turning the pages, commenting on each one. Some of them were bad, the heart-lipped beauties in profile we all tried once in a while in math clsss, a few tired magnolias, some lop-sided buildings; but then I got to the animals. Round, furred kittens that you knew were going to grow into cats. Zoo monkeys, hanging on the bars, pretending to be people. Fat pigeons strutting among cigarette wrappers on their way to drop white splatters on Robert E. Lee.

I glanced up at her. She was watching me with the hungry expression I had seen on her mother at the door. "These are good." I couldn't keep the surprise out of my voice.

"Do you think so?" She waited to lap up my praise, her mouth parted and her plump cheeks blushing a little.

I nodded, turning to the animals again, telling her what I thought about each one. I don't know how long we were there when she said, "I guess we'd better go down." I hadn't heard anything, but she carefully closed the book and placed it on her desk.

Her mother was at the foot of the stairs waiting for us. There was a tight pulled look at the corners of her mouth. "What time is it, dear?" she said with that glittering, bird-sharp voice.

I saw the hall clock behind her in a brass star. The shiny brass hands had just slipped off each other and were pointing to 3:20.

"I can't imagine what has happened." Her voice slivered a little.

"You live pretty far out," I said, the excuse sounding pretty bad even to me.

She nodded abstractedly. "I suppose so." Then she added, "I'd better see about the ice cream."

She bustled off and Jan and I stood aimlessly at the foot of the stairs. I could see the pink crepe paper through the door of the dining room.

The silence lengthened uncomfortably and the hall clock pinged 3:30.

"You want to go in the back yard?" Jan said at last.

"Okay."

We trudged through the kitchen. Her mother was standing beside the refrigerator where I guessed she had just checked the cartons of ice cream. "You two go on outside. I'll be here to catch the door." Her voice was brittle, like overdone candy cracking on a plate.

I thought as we filed past that it would be better if she went up to take a nap and could have the excuse later of maybe having missed the knocker. It was getting awfully late.

We went out back and took turns sitting on the swing in the oak tree they had out back and I told her about the book I was reading. I didn't much want to share it, but I had to talk about something. I told her she could have it after I finished even though I had intended to let my best friend Aileen read it next so we could make up joint Foreign Legion daydreams. We rocked back and forth a while, not really swinging, just sort of waiting and trying to limp along in a kind of conversation. I knew we were both listening, straining to hear a knock, a footstep on the sidewalk out front.

Her mother appeared at the back screen. "I thought you girls would like a preview lemonade. It's so hot this afternoon."

"It really is," I agreed hastily. She somehow made me feel awful. I guess it was the word "preview" that did it. As if there were really going to be something to follow, the birthday party when the other thirty-one guests arrived. "Pink lemonade sounds great." I hadn't meant to say "pink."

She gave a little stilted laugh and I couldn't tell if she noticed. "It's all made."

We waited and took turns in the swing until she brought the two glasses out on a little tray. I saw her coming from the corner of my eye and said, "I bet you can't guess what I got for your birthday."

Jan shook her head, looking at me sort of grinning.

"It's something to wear," I said prolonging it. Then as her mother got there with the lemonade, I looked up, startled, as if I hadn't seen her. "That looks good," I said a little too loudly at the pink liquid. There wasn't any ice in it; the freezer part of their box was probably full of ice cream.

She strained out a smile. I thought I saw her lower lip quiver a little.

"I got so hot coming out here. I didn't know you lived so near the end of the trolley line." I tried to put over the idea of distance and maybe a confusion about their address. "This is great." I took a quick sip.

"Really great," Jan chorused.

But her mother was already on her way back to the kitchen, into the house where she'd be able to hear the door.

We stayed there in the hot shade, alternately leaning against the rough tree trunk and sitting in the swing until I guessed it must have been about four o'clock or so. We were still listening too hard to talk much.

"Want something to eat?"

I couldn't face that pink dining room with the crepe paper streamers and the thirty-three nut cups. I hesitated.

She must have understood. "We have some cupcakes, in case we ran out of . . . ." Her voice trailed off.

"Fine, I love cupcakes," I said hurriedly.

As we came in her mother came from the front of the house.

"We thought we'd have a cupcake," Jan said.

"Oh, yes. That's a fine idea," she began. "And have a dip of the ice . . . ." Then her face crumpled like a sheet of wadded paper. Her lips wavered over the word and a great sob hiccuped through her throat. She put her hand over her mouth as she turned and ran toward the hall, and I saw her back heaving as she disappeared beside the stairs.

We pretended we hadn't seen anything. Jan got the little pink cakes from a bin and dished out two great heaps of strawberry ice cream, and we stood beside the sink and ate them.

I had separate sensations of dry warmish crumbs and iced smoothness passing across my tongue, but I couldn't taste anything. But I ate the little cake and the bowl of ice cream and when she offered me another cupcake and more ice cream, I took them and ate them too.

I repeated some of my compliments about her sketches and added more as I thought of them and spooned up the chopped bits of strawberry in the bottom of the dish. We dragged out the ritual until shadows began to ease into the kitchen and I saw by the kitchen clock that it was after 5:30. I told her I had better leave to be able to get home before dark with such a long trolley ride back uptown. "Tell your mother," I began, but I couldn't think what she should tell her mother for me and I stopped.

As we went toward the front door I saw the pink paper of the dining room glowing in the afternoon sun.

"See you Monday. I'll bring the book," I said loudly at the front door.

She waved her hand and shut the door. The knot of balloons jogged, settled lightly against one another beneath the pink satin ribbon on the door knocker as I went down the sidewalk.

MISS AMELIA'S

IT WAS RAINING a fine, light mist of New Orleans rain when she unlocked the door, carefully, quietly, even though no one else was there. She was always the first one there, had been the one to open the shop door at 9 A.M. exactly every weekday morning since 1933 when Miss Amelia's father first gave her the second key to the alley door, and she'd never missed a single day but her vacations in all those years except for the week she took off in addition to her vacation two years back when her mother passed away. Died, she corrected herself softly the way the psychiatrist had said it over and over to get her used to the fact that their mother was gone, hers and Albert's gone from the house just down the street from the shop, the beautiful old antebellum house so set back in the brick patio that no one could see from the sidewalk, that no one had been in but the two of them since their mother had passed, died.

She turned on the light with the overhead fan that was on the same switch, glanced around, and frowned. Some of the pieces had been moved. From the time she'd left last night the Queen Anne table had been put over against the wall, and the 1690 carved chair had been taken out of the front window and replaced by an ordinary butterscotch Lincoln rocker.

It was disgraceful. As if someone switched your home around after you'd gone to bed, turning the place upside down, moving the fine old pieces as if they were any old furniture. Miss Amelia should have known better than to hire that bunch of . . . . She couldn't think of a word for them. Bunch of useless, trifling . . . . She sighed, unable to name what they were, the whole lot of them. But Miss Amelia, even in the present state of her affairs, should have known better.

They didn't have regard for the pieces, dragging sandpaper over the wood with no feeling for it, slapping paint or stain on careless, casual, working for the $2 an hour without any respect, any notion of what they were working on.

She started to make the coffee, lighting the gas ring with the kitchen matches she always brought from home when they ran out, favoring her shoulder, trying not to touch it and make it start needing a massage. The rain always made her arthritis worse, and Brother was saying just the other night while they were watching television that the . . . .

"Morning."

She glanced up from the coffee pot and nodded, tightened without answering.

It was one of them, the boy who did the gluing and repairing, sometimes a bit of the carving, but whose name she hadn't bothered to sort out from the others. They stayed one or two years, then they were gone, and she'd only have to learn new ones.

"I see that maple set's ready for staining, eh?"

"Yes." He didn't do the staining. It wasn't his place to comment on the work the others were supposed to be doing. That's what had changed so. When the colored man Woodrow used to come in, he did exactly what he was told to do and there wasn't any of this.

"Man, look at this rain!" Another one of them came through the door, his long hair in a club at the back of his neck. He closed the door too hard and the old glass shivered, the gilt letters S'AILEMA wavering slightly, settling, and he shook himself like a wet furred animal, shaking drops off the lank of hair that dotted, blistered up on a table top near the door.

"The weatherman said it'd let up by noon," the other one said.

They laughed as if he'd said something funny, and she went in the back room.

The pitted old pedestal table stood where she'd left it and she patted it softly as she went by to get the sandpaper box, carefully portioning out two new sheets of paper that would last her the day, tearing them in quarters to stretch them. That girl who came in the afternoons was always using new paper on every piece, rubbing away for a little while with a square and then getting herself another, wasting sandpaper that could be used again and again if you were frugal.

She wrapped the sandpaper over a blackboard eraser and started rubbing slowly on the table top. The eraser always reminded her of going to school that first day with Brother. No matter how many times she picked one up and wrapped it with sandpaper to use on the flat smooth surfaces, that day was always in the side of her consciousness, waiting for her to catch a glimpse of it and see it whole as if they were children once more and her mother was standing at the wrought iron patio gate watching them walk down Ru Royal to the corner where the Ursuline Sisters had thei school, both of them looking over their shoulders and waving back every few steps until they got to the corner and had to turn and blot out the sight of their mother back at the gate. And how she took Brother to his room, older and important when he was just starting, to come back for him at lunch, only to discover on their way home that he had an eraser in his back pocket, stuffed there because he thought they were supposed to take them with them when they left the blackboard. How many times they'd laughed about that, little Albert with the fuzzy eraser sticking out of his knickers' back pocket, and her so horrified at his stealing from the Sisters. How they'd laughed later, she and Brother and Mother.

"Did you want this sanded down with the 220 paper next?"

She hadn't seen him come in and she clinched herself closed against him. "I'm doing this table." It was one piece she could keep from them.

He shrugged and went over to the paint cabinet for the stain and brush, started on the Duncan Phyfe set in the cleared space at the back. She watched him out of the corner of her eye. She didn't do any painting or staining any longer. They kept changing the names of the paints, Salem Maple, Parchment, Asian Black Mahogany, Honey Beige, Fruitwood. There weren't any simple ones any more and she couldn't keep the names straight, couldn't remember what strange label went with what wood any longer.

She sanded slowly, pausing to run her fingers over the wood that was becoming smooth, polished like bone.

Maybe if the Crash hadn't come when it did and all the money gone so fast and complete, she could have stayed on with the Sisters to . . . .

"Whose cigarette is this?" Miss Amelia stood in the center of the shop holding a lighted cigarette between her thumb and forefinger as if her fingers were pincers, tweezers to hold it away from her. "I want to know!" Her voice was half between a shout and a scream, anger and frustration pressing up from beneath like bubbled veneer, but even sharp edged as it was you could still tell she was one of the New Orleans Beaujolais.

They all looked up but no one answered.

It was just one more thing from them, she thought. She'd heard them talk and knew they were all afraid of Miss Amelia, but then they didn't understand about her.

"You stupid bastards have got to watch it."

She always winced when Miss Amelia used those terms, but the Beaujolais always were so high strung.

"The wood in these damned old places is like straw. A little fire in here with all this paint and turpentine would make this whole goddamn block of Royal go up."

Miss Amelia should get rid of the lot of them, she thought again and turned back to her sanding, easing her shoulder as she worked.

She glanced occasionally at the clock. Brother came home at twelve sharp, and he always liked having his cold lunch on the table as he walked through the door. It had been so much easier when Mother was alive and still able to do a few things around the house, but now she always had to leave by a quarter of twelve to get home in time to dish up his cottage cheese and slice his tomatoes. It was a wonder he never got tired of them for lunch every day of the year, but he insisted that now he'd turned fifty he had to have one meal that was diet and he always insisted on his potatoes and french bread for dinner.

When it was almost noon, the rain was still coming down, a thick veiled rain that weighted the magnolia leaves and ran in wide rivulets down the bricked alley. Even going two doors down she was soaked through.

And by the time she'd changed her wet things, Brother was already in the kitchen drying his face with a tea towel and stolidly eyeing the unset table.

"I'm a little late today because of the rain."

He didn't answer and she knew he was going to give her that silent treatment of his she felt so much more keenly since the loss of her mother who knew how to get him out of it.

"It's difficult working all shut in with the paint smells," she said doggedly, trying not to notice his silence, bustling, laying out the luncheon things, trying to appease him. "And Miss Amelia yelling at every little thing until it makes your head ache. You know how she always was a nervous girl, but now that her husband's in Mandeville after eating that glass." She looked up. "And it's such a gloomy day."

He went into the parlor, but when she called him and the cold lunch was on the table, he came back and his face had cleared. They sat down and he even passed her the crackers first.

"Did you have a nice morning, dear?"

"In all this rain?" he said crossly.

But it was at least an answer. And she told him about how someone had moved the furniture around the evening before, trying to take over the shop and how someone had left a cigarette that could have caught the place on fire just like that, and how the young, she paused and added, young ruffians weren't careful with the pieces and didn't seem even to care about them.

"You talk about all that furniture as if it was alive, Sister," he said lifting a great forkful of cottage cheese.

She smiled, embarrassed. "Well, it almost is," she laughed a little breathlessly. Every time he kidded her she felt herself blushing. She knew it was silly, but she did think of them as individuals, as separate entities, one of a kind because of the nicks, gouges, scratches that made each chair different from the others no matter how many were in a set.

But she was glad he was in a better mood.

On her way back to the shop she remembered to take an umbrella and went around to the front door to avoid all the soaked leaves of the back patio.

Miss Amelia looked out the little office alcove while she was closing the umbrella.

"Come in a minute." Miss Amelia had the same frown she always wore, but her voice was lower than usual.

She felt a sudden timidness. She hadn't stopped and talked to Miss Amelia in she couldn't remember how long.

"Sit down."

There was a lovely old love seat upholstered in wine against the wall and she sat on it shyly.

"You're almost sixty now, aren't you?" Miss Amelia had a pencil in her hand and tapped the point on a stack of wrinkled order sheets.

Miss Amelia was exactly ten years younger to the week, and she knew how old they both were.

"I've been thinking it's about time you gave yourself a rest." Miss Amelia got up and tugged at her paint-stained sweater, pulled her hand over the mannish-cut graying hair. "You've been working in this shop for forty years. You were here before my father died, back when my Harold was . . . ," she broke off. "I think it's about time you took a rest."

"But I don't want a rest," she began breathlessly.

"You can't do the staining any longer or the repair work, and even the sanding's getting hard for you to manage." Miss Amelia's voice was getting rougher, furred like plank wood.

"But I don't . . . ."

"This kind of work takes someone younger." Miss

Amelia sat down at the rolltop desk and picked up the pencil again. "This shop is all I've got left. It's got to pay. I can't keep a . . . ." She didn't look up. "Next week show one of the boys how to order coffee from the Morning Call and how to use that antique coffee pot and gas ring out in back."

She got up off the love seat, moving without noticing, out the office door, back into the work room.

She'd been all her life in the shop. She'd never thought of leaving it. Ever since she finished school and the convent and . . . it was really more hers than Miss Amelia's who had been too young to help for so many years and who took summers off for buying trips to Europe, weeks off at a time with that husband of hers. Not Miss Amelia but she was the one who'd stayed with the shop, worked, watched the pieces become shining, glowing, refinished elegance, ready to go into good homes, ready for people who wanted fine old things. In forty-three years thousands of pieces had been transformed beneath her hands that loved the stroke of their polished wood.

It must be another of Miss Amelia's moods. What with her troubles at home and of course being worried to death about Harold. Miss Amelia probably would've forgotten all about it by Monday.

But when it was five, quitting time every Friday, Miss Amelia came into the painting area with her raincoat.

"Give your key to Brad here next week." Her hand indicated one of the boys who looked like all the others although his reddish hair was bushier, more frizzled about his head than any of the others. "He can start getting up early enough to open up if he's not too hung over."

Miss Amelia was telling her to go.

She'd never thought about it, never conceived, imagined such a possibility. She put away her things without being aware of the others, without noticing what she was doing, shutting up the sandpaper, the steel wool, the eraser automatically, mechanically.

She was vaguely aware that the others had gone as she closed and locked the back door, but she put up the umbrella not realizing the rain had stopped.

If she could only talk it over with Mother. She peeled the potatoes and put on the pan to boil. Brother insisted on fresh boiled potatoes no matter if they were to be mashed even though once she tried the boxed kind and was sure if he hadn't seen the package he never could have told the difference. The shop had become as much hers as Miss Amelia's. She hadn't even considered . . . .

"Whew, what a day." Brother came in from the front and dropped into a kitchen chair, began taking off his shoes and socks, curling his plump toes against the linoleum just like when he was a little boy.

He told her about how they brought in a whole file drawer an hour before quitting time and how he made damn sure all those girls stayed until they got it all sorted out, and she smiled brightly and went on fixing his dinner.

When it was ready she managed to eat a few bites but she couldn't taste anything, and she sat through the programs Brother picked without noticing what was on. And when Brother switched off the set, she went to bed as numbly, lay staring at the darkness, the patio light glazing the magnolia leaves beside her window.

It wasn't until the next night, in the same unchanging blackness with the same unchanged patterns on the glistening leaves and ceiling of her room, that she knew what she had to do.

After she knew for certain, she was calm, refreshed, and the next morning she could laugh at Brother's crooked tie that she straightened as they went to church. But during the day she became a little on edge, impatient with the heat, excited with a first day of the new school year feeling. She hoped Brother wouldn't notice anything and was relieved when he turned off the television and went to bed.

Then she changed from her Sunday dress with the tiny silk flowers and put on the clothes she wore to work. It was a hot night, the air heavy and still, and she went out cautiously not to disturb Brother, went into the alley to the back of the shop.

She unlocked the door and switched on the light, hearing the fan whir with the brightness.

She held her breath and looked around.

The fine old pedestal table, the carved 1690 chair, the deacon's bench, an arrow-back rocker that still needed gluing, an old wooden icebox like the one they'd had at home for so many years, the gold lettering on the front door that she could see from where she stood.

She went to the cabinet, her hands shaking, and took out a five gallon can of acetone. She eased the lid and then uncapped it, set it in the middle of the floor. She dumped out the box of staining rags, some clotted with paint, some almost clean, and got the box of kitchen matches. She carefully pushed over the can with her foot and watched the acetone pour onto the rags, some of it soaking over into her canvas shoe. The instant cold of the liquid on her foot made her shiver. She was so excited she could hardly breathe.

She looked up once more at her table not yet finished, its oak top not yet sealed or laquered, not yet gleaming. Then she took out two matches, struck them together, and dropped them on the pile of rags.

SUNDAY MORNING

"JUST TAKE IT easy. It doesn't hurt that much."

His voice was suave, calm, practiced.

The pain welled out, radiating, cutting her in half so sharply, so abruptly that her breath stopped. There was nothing but the white pain filling her, consuming her. Then it started receding, drawing back into itself somewhere inside that was not a part of her, and she remembered that she wasn't supposed to hold her breath, that she was supposed to pant like a dog instead.

"Now see."

He put his hand heavily on the white swathed mound and she felt it and knew it was a part of her he was touching, something that had belonged to her but somehow didn't any more.

She moved her ankles against the straps, the metal against her heels, but she couldn't see them over the mound.

It started again.

She knew she could stand it, she was prepared for it, and she remembered to open her mouth and take in the short choppy bits of air. But it was worse than she'd thought as it swelled, carrying her with it behind her closed eyelids and passed what she could stand.

"Just relax," the nurse said from somewhere outside the pain. "They're coming along nicely now, doctor."

It went down again, lowering her with it onto a glass shelf. But she'd tensed against it and she was stiff.

"Breathe, breathe. That's the girl."

She should concentrate on relaxing the next time it came, telling herself it couldn't win, but a woman was screaming through a wall in the next cubicle, and she couldn't close out the sound enough to think herself calm.

"Listen to the one Dr. Davis got," the nurse said.

As it started, a hand pressed down on the mound and it fought against the hand, sharpening itself, breaking her in two. She wanted to push the hand away, but both of hers were strapped down and she could only move her head from side to side.

Breathe, breathe, pant like a dog next time.

She didn't know if it was actually worse or if she was merely giving in to it a little more each time, letting it swallow her, melt away a little more of her, feed on her from inside, grow each time.

When it recoiled, she wouldn't be blind and could focus, hear their voices.

She didn't know how long it had been coming, receding, its swells of brilliant pain sweeping her up, out, faster, the lowerings shorter, almost without a chance to pause. She lost contact with time and her arms and legs knotted into clenched muscles.

Then "I see the head coming," he said.

But somehow that didn't mean anything in the grip of the terrible grinding pain. She tried to rise above it, to breathe, but she couldn't find the rim of it and her lungs wouldn't work around it.

"Push now."

Again and again, faster, one swell coming before the last had quite gone down. Moans were close around her and she felt the clamminess of her forehead like blood.

"Push!"

She had to defecate but the pain clamped around her and it was as if her insides were crashing through the partition of her bowels.

"There!"

A great rushing, bursting shattered the glass shelf.

"There," one of them said again.

It receded again and a hand touched her. It had gone down enough for her to open her eyelids.

He was holding up a baby. A slick blue yellow body, long and lifeless, a narrow and hairless animal.

Then he slapped his hand against it and the body quivered, took a breath that washed through it in a pink flood and changed the yellow. It let the breath out again in a fierce cry.

He gave it to the nurse who began busily wiping it at another table as the pain started again.

She gasped and was betrayed. It hadn't ended. She moaned.

"That's the afterbirth coming now," he said complacently and put his hand on the white mound again.

She looked at it startled even over the pain. It hadn't gone down, hadn't changed at all and yet the baby was already out. But then she could see it ripple, looser than it had been, sway as the pain came and went, lessening, lessening.

"Do you feel that?"

He was sitting at the foot of the table below the mound and she couldn't see him.

She waited to see if there was anything to feel. "No."

"I'm sewing you up now, but I didn't think you'd feel anything. Usually the pressure of the head has deadened everything."

He went on talking and she could see the long rough strand pull up in a hemming motion as he sewed.

Her muscles ached with excruciating stiffness and the waves of pain were still coming, going. But it had weakened, it was over and she knew it.

The woman next door was still moaning.

They had taken the baby away and she realized she hadn't asked what it was. That didn't seem to matter somehow.

Without interest she let them do whatever they were doing. She lay racked, waiting.

Finally they released her ankles and wrists, but the cramps didn't go away immediately as she'd thought they would. The nurse brought another stiff new sheet and recovered, rearranged her. They put a needle in her arm and hooked it to colorless tubes that ran to a colorless liquid in a bottle above her head.

"There we are."

In a bright glare of lights two white suited men wheeled her out into the hallway.

Whitney was there and pressed her hand with his until her bones hurt. He was smiling, patting her hand all the way down the hall to the room.

The baby was already there in a white bassinet laced with a blue ribbon over the top and she wondered if that meant it was a boy.

They wheeled her next to it, rolled her and the colorless tubes onto the hospital bed there beside the bassinet, covered her with the stiff sheet and a white cotton spread.

"Is this ours?" He was peering down into the curve of the bassinet.

It wasn't, it was hers, but she looked over, not to have to say it, looking toward but not really seeing the baby, and nodded.

PROGRESS REPORT—
CANDELARIA PROJECT

I STOOD AT the mud-baked window casing, staring into the sun crackling heat and hating them.

Their pretense at industry, their guilty droop of the neck, and their opaque eyes as they slowly unloaded the back of the jeep. It took two of them to lift each cardboard carton of the powdered milk and carry it gingerly down the jeep ramp and through the door held open by a third man. Only those three were actually working; the rest of the town crowded around the jeep, watching with their blank dulled eyes. I saw one of the men trace out the lettering on the side of the jeep with his filthy forefinger. I don't know how many thousands of times he had spelled out the words, yet now with deep concentration his slack lips mouthed the Spanish and then the English. "Universidad del Valle." He lip read slowly. "Rockefeller Foundation." Even more slowly.

The sun on the white enamel of the jeep hurt my eyes, and I turned away from the window. Sun blotches danced over the room; my retina spread a black mirage over the desk before the second of fancy faded and the sun spots evaporated. A catheter in an aluminum pan had been carefully centered on a stack of papers, carefully and squarely, the way a child might place it, with the pan's weight crumpling a sheet of typed report, creasing the paper into irreparable folds.

I looked at the ruined sheet. To hell with it.

I sat down heavily in the wooden desk chair and shifted against the straight back. The hide seat bristled through my slacks. So it would take them all afternoon to unload one jeep full of CARE powdered milk with the entire village watching. So what.

I'd been at it six months. Six eternal months of commuting from Cali every day over dust roads to the dust village of sun-baked streets, sun-dried adobe hospital, sun-cracked mud huts, sun-dried brick cathedral with its double steeples and its scratched record of bells for matins and vespers. Six eternal months of heat and dry rottenness and bone curvature and skin eruptions on babies whose mothers fed them rice water from the cook pots because they and the rest of the forsaken village know that mother's milk is unhealthy for newborns. Six months of explanations, pleadings, exhortations, re-explanations, and the culmination in that pitiful little plot of vegetable seeds I had stuck into the dry flaking earth while I explained once more about the milk and the vegetables for children, hoping that once, only once, I could see some flutter of interest or understanding.

And they had watched me dig the little furrows and cover the dry seeds with the dry gritty earth, had watched me with their lusterless eyes, blankly, with careless sweat staining their cotton shirts, had watched me beneath the cloudless violent sky and had lounged against the wooden fence with palpable indifference.

Now I had the CARE milk, the 312 cardboard boxes to be

delivered to the little adobe hospital every month so that the families, loosely called, could have milk for their rickety children. And who gave a damn.

A fly whirred through the cutout adobe square that served as a window and joined others of his species along the wide crack in the white-washed adobe ceiling. The two rooms of beds that served as wards and the single room of consultation and/or operation had screens and a screen door that slammed off the rest of the tiny hospital, but the offices had only eaves to block the yellow shafts of sun and the daily tropical showers that dropped without warning in afternoon regularity and then evaporated as suddenly in the drying sunlight.

"Doctora?"

"Sí?"

I looked down from the crack in the ceiling. One of the men was standing at the door with his neck curved slightly and his head hanging down as he talked in his soft Spanish. "Doctora, el jeep está listo." He didn't look at me directly but at the desk and the shiny aluminum pan holding the catheter.

"Está bien," I said trying to put some enthusiasm in my voice. It didn't work. I could see his neck bend a fraction of a centimeter lower; his eyes shifted to his grimy hands. "That will be all for today then since it is Pascuas," I added, "You may tell the men gracias for their help."

"Sí, doctora." He stood hesitant another second then turned abruptly and vanished.

I looked at the empty doorway. My seven years in Turkey hadn't seemed as long as these six months in Colombia. I stood up and resisted the impulse to move the aluminum pan from its crush of papers and to smooth out the typed report.

To drive back to Cali was the usual dust-filled jog over

hard dirt clots to the highway and into the spreading city, past wavering cyclists, burros with racks of cane on their ulcerated sides, porcelain-eyed bystanders with empty, aimless hands, past Juanchito and its flimsy scrap hovels oozing in diseased rows toward the river, beneath the bridge. Tiny bloated children, wearing only shrunken vests, waddling to the doorways watching. I caught glimpses of moist blueberry eyes, enlarged round eyes that had not yet dried in the sun-baked country to a stare of opaque hopelessness.

The drive was usual until I reached Avenida de las Americas. There I hit the Pascuas crowds and the Good Friday funeral procession. Measured steps to the tempo of a hollow drum, slow moving black suits tailored from a 1920 pattern, a scattering of humped women in black with handkerchiefs over their weeping eyes.

From the height of the jeep cab I could see the body. A prone, life-sized Christ beneath a massive gilded crown of thorns. The pale enameled face carved into agony, the glass eyes crossed in infinite interior pain, the swelling veins bursting through the wooden hands. The image of a dead god, wrapped in thick plum velvet, enclosed in polished glass.

I sat in the jeep and watched them with their sunlit illusion merging into sweaty reality as they wept behind the body. I'd never be able to fathom them, not in six more months or six more years. I'd never be able to reach them. The slow beat on the loosened drumhead pounded in my temples as the procession slowly turned into Calle Sexta.

The last of the mourners filed past, and I turned the jeep off the avenue, across a yellowed bridge to the other side of the Rio Cali. On this side of the river lay shaded, iron-barred residences and the homeless poor who camped on the river bank and begged at the ironed, barred doors for rice. As I crossed the yellowed bridge, I saw two women thigh deep in the water pounding at the gauze of what had once been a cotton shirt. Without soap they bent down and hammered dirt from the cloth with a river stone. A naked child on the bank was carefully spreading other bits of ragged bedding over the grass to dry. None of them looked up.

I shifted gears and pushed the jeep up the incline where my apartment hung, its balcony jutting brow-like from the side of the building. On this side of the river, up away from the water, there was only hot dry silence. Silence and potent sunlight and the full lipped blossoms of yellow raintrees.

I braked and sat in the hot jeep, unwilling to climb the brilliantly scrubbed stairs to my apartment and the waiting muchacho. I knew there would be muchacho for dinner, Good Friday or not. Its thick beef muscle stuffed with onions and bacon and surrounded by glutinous masses of rice and boiled plantain. Teresa, my maid-cook, always had muchacho on Friday because, I suspected, I ate very little of it, and there was always plenty left for Saturday when her younger sister came.

The moist boiled smell of it hung over the apartment as I opened the door.

Teresa was sweeping the marble floor with futile broom strokes, brushing what lint and dust she could without undue effort onto a folded newspaper. Then she would turn back the rug and mop the white marble. Carefully, mechanically, mindlessly, as she did every afternoon, Easter weekend or not. Sunlight slanted across her fat back as she bent over her paper and broom. She glanced up and nodded without warmth, "Buenas tardes, doctora."

I raised a hand and nodded, continuing to the upper floor that was equally full of the beef smell. A thick meat odor that clung to the drapes and my few silk party dresses.

I found the mejorales and tossed down a couple with a swallow of tap water, which, thanks to an American engineer some thirty years ago, was potable in Cali if nowhere else in the country. The powdered grit clung to my throat, but even Colombians couldn't seem to ruin the simple aspirin.

Then I jerked off my sweaty drill shirt and slacks that would be beaten unmercifully against the tiled patio sink in the morning. I dumped them into the hamper, briefly considering mentioning one more time to Teresa that soap would be sufficient. Then I shrugged and splashed tepid water over my face. Why bother?

I got through the meal as quickly as possible and escaped into the silent, darkened street. There were other Americans in the building across the street, but I didn't feel like talking to them. No one could be as sick of Colombia and its lethargic people as I was at that moment, and I was in no mood for any other gringo's small tribulations.

I walked slowly down the hill from one patch of street-light to the next and crossed the dark footbridge. There was little to fear from night marauders in Cali itself. Empty house robbery and unobtrusive pick-pocketry were a daily vocation, but Caleños seemed as inept at actual face to face thievery or rape as they were at most things; as far as I knew no one had ever even reported a holdup.

From the bridge the next puddle of light was Aqui Es Miguel's, the little restaurant bar where Cali's serenaders stayed between jobs, where they waited patiently, without seeming to care one way or the other, for contracts.

I dropped into a chair near the pink neon sign and held up my fingers to the waiter for an aguardiente. He knew me and had ceased to think it strange that I often came in alone. I didn't like aguardiente particularly, but it was available, inexpensive, and quick, and I felt the need for a border of alcoholic padding to tolerate the hot, infested country one more night.

A soft wash sounded from the river, and the pale blue illumination of the three crosses rose in distant solitude opposite me.

"Señora." He brought the tiny shot glass of viscous, transparent liquid and a small dish of orange slices for the leisurely drinker who sipped and nibbled oranges. I pushed the dish away and gulped the liquid in one swallow, holding my breath. The licorice flavor came into my mouth only after I had set the glass carefully back into its own sticky ring on the table top.

Around me in isolated oblivion the serenaders plucked at their guitar strings and hummed separate laments. There were no other patrons. It was early yet for the Caleños.

The grease spattered waiter brought me two more aguardientes, and then another as I emptied the tiny glasses and set them in a straight row diagonally across the table top.

Already there was a faint dizziness in the air, in the pink neon haze.

On my sixth glass the ubiquitous fireworks began. In the black sky, arching above the hill of the three crosses, a brilliant green dot of light curved upward, then broke apart, falling in green slow motion, dusting the hill and the pale luminous crosses. A red dot followed the lazy curve into the darkness to drift downward in brilliant fragments. Then another green, a second red. For all holidays they had to have candles and fireworks, ephemeral and useless. La pyrotecnica, colorful, worthless. I looked away.

I allotted myself one more sickly sweet glass as the plop of the fireworks punctuated the night river, then I began the walk back across the footbridge, back up the lamp-dotted slope. The liqueur had done nothing to alleviate my disgust, my irritation that embraced the hot, barred houses along the hill.

I fumbled with the key in the glare of the porch light,

burning to discourage night thieves, and climbed to the meat perfumed bedroom.

After two more mejorales I slipped off the cotton shift and got into the already warm bed.

It woke me when it hit. I hadn't heard any thunder, but in the blackness I had an impression of rupturing sky and clouds. And then great enveloping masses of rain that curled like woven matting around the house and formed an impenetrable wall of water between me and the street lamp below, not falling, but filling the air with twisted rows of water.

I propped myself up on my elbows to watch it waver from the darkness into the yellow light and break into a thousand refractions with an endlessness that seemed immobile. A flood, a true Spanish lluvia.

I watched it, feeling stifled, surrounded, insulated in a water casing, then lay back on my propped damp pillow with the taste of licorice coating my tongue. My bedside clock read 2:35.

The next morning the rain still filled the sky, the air, the branches, the sodden blossoms of the golden raintrees. The sponge of the tropical earth had absorbed water until it too had become colloidal. A swollen brown flood washed down the hill past the jeep, the brown swirling water covering the naked hubs whose caps had been stolen two months before.

A great block of rain waited outside the door like a waterfall. Beneath a battered umbrella I waded to the jeep and felt the rivered street rush past, foaming about my knees, as I climbed drenched into the high jeep cab.

I had intended staying at the clinic until at least noon, and here I was already wet to the knees. I debated briefly whether or not to make the drive, but the rain hammering on the metal jeep roof decided me and I turned the key.

The jeep floated slightly backward with the water, then began to move. The windshield hit the heavy drops that seemed suspended in the air. The engine labored, and the wipers dragged across the glass, stirring but not affecting the water mass outside.

The crystalline blindness persisted through the hazed city that slid past the jeep windows. I switched on the lights and concentrated on finding the street.

Once out of town, I slowed to see the turnoff to Candelaria and jerked onto it at the last second. The jeep skidded, and I fought to keep it on the road I could feel without seeing. Great waves sprayed past each side of the jeep that lurched against the water inertia.

And still the rain continued.

At last the twin-steepled church and the little adobe clinic resolved, dissolved, then formed again in the gray water sky and earth. There was no one in sight.

They at least seemed to have sense enough to stay in out of the rain.

I leaped from the jeep to the little clinic's screen door, shook off the umbrealla and wet raincoat, wiped a paper towel across my hair. I should have stayed dry in Cali. I wadded the coarse wet paper towel and tossed it away. No one would venture to the clinic in torrents like this no matter what his illness. Not a Colombian.

While I was still standing there, musing at but not really focusing on the rain outside, I heard soft padding footsteps down the hall.

"Doctora?"

One of the villagers stood in the doorway. I had forgotten his name. His cotton shirt and trousers were plastered to his skin. Water streamed down his hair, dripped from his earlobes, his nose, stubbled chin. Dirty puddles formed around his dark bare feet. His brown eyes were the only thing dry about him.

"Doctora?" he repeated as if he hadn't spoken before.
"Sí?"

He looked drenched but not sick. "Puede venir, doctora?" He pointed with his dripping water crinkled hand.

I nodded. "Sí." I assumed a wife. "Su esposa?"

He shook his head, flicking water like a wet dog, and turned toward the door. "No, doctora."

We hit the rain once more. It sucked out my breath as if someone had punched me on the back. He didn't seem affected. I followed him behind the clinic.

He led me to the garden.

As we sloshed through the narrow gate I could see them in the gray sheafs of rain. Almost the entire village. Standing with pieces of sack, they were hovering over the tiny rows of seedlings, shielding the little plants with their bodies and their bits of cloth, protecting as best they could the minute growth of vegetables I had planted. I could see the little canals they had dug to guide the water from the rows toward the ditches they had cut along the fence.

The rain had started at 2:35. They must have come in the black morning rain. All of them. With their scraps of sacking and their hands to protect the garden.

"Está bien, doctora?" A gentle voice came from the rain-filled air.

I stood looking at them, feeling the cool rain wash over me. Their eyes beneath drenched black hair were studiously on the ground and the water that covered their bare feet. I nodded slowly. "Está bien."

THE PEEPING TOM

THE SNOW WAS softly crushing the dead world outside,
drifting past the windows in great forgotten spirals. The
cabbage-rosed linoleum was slick as ice and as cold and she
touched the ball of her foot to it, the pad of flesh shrinking
back but soothed. The ache lessened, numbed, and she put
her foot back in the laceless man's shoe that had turned cold
as the floor.

If I could just touch him once more.

That curve between the bulges of his deep chest, hollow
like a valley, flowering, tangling with black hair.

Just once more.

"But you wasn't meant to," she said aloud, not too loud,
but firm. "It wasn't meant to be."

It was usually only when she worked late at night that she
got to thinking about it, and she'd taken to talking to herself
then, not much and full aware she was doing it, but talking

some in the winter night silence, after the kids were down, while she was doing ironing for the women in camp.

She'd felt almost guilty taking in the ironing at first, knowing they were giving up their laundry baskets of clothes to let her have some way of living through the winter, giving her some way of earning, and she knew they were giving up their own evening's work for her, knew they were sitting home trying to find other things to keep busy.

She put the cooled flatiron on the stove top, unhooked it and caught another hot one on the handle. The seams of the iron stove glowed red with the wood fire.

A telegram called in from Thermopolis to the office and then typed out, not like in the movies with cut and pasted words, but typed out neat on a piece of white paper, was probably the best way. She'd seen Sarah Trewitt at her husband's funeral after he'd been blown up in the rig blast and she'd thought then that if anything happened to Royce she'd probably do the same, want them to open the casket one more time before they put it in the ground. Maybe not throwing herself across it the way Sarah did, but maybe wanting to. It was better this way. They wrote they'd ship the body back after the war and then of course there'd be no way of opening it.

The phone jangled harsh across the stillness, rough, metallic.

She paused over the slick white of the shirt sleeve to count.

Four rings for the Smithers. It was certainly late for anyone to be calling the Smithers. She said mechanically that she hoped it wasn't anything serious, warding off the serious by saying it.

She went back to the sleeve before the flatiron cooled. No one else in camp could do fresh starched white shirts like she did and she didn't feel guilty any more about them, it was only the handkerchiefs and napkins and little girl's puffed sleeved dresses that anyone could do.

The phone rang again. Three rings for the Howards.

Who in the world would be calling all around camp so late.

She hadn't heard the schoolhouse bell, and she knew the sound would have jarred her into noticing it no matter what she'd been doing. As far as she knew nobody in camp ever missed the schoolhouse bell.

And then came the two rings for her.

She was expecting them and yet not, and the silence that fell after the second short ring made her stomach and her chest tighten, lurch involuntarily. She was breathless like she'd walked through the snow to get there when she took down the receiver.

"Hello." She leaned into the black mouthpiece, tugging at it out of nervousness to pull it down even though it was already set for her mouth height.

"Cora?" But then Gladys's voice didn't wait for an answer. "I'm calling to warn everybody in camp there's a Peeping Tom out. They seen him last night and again tonight."

"A what?"

"You know, one of them guys that peeks in windows at people. Ella Connors seen somebody lookin' in at the Kelloggs last night, and then tonight Doc Wilson thought there was someone outside his own house. There was footprints all around like the guy wanted a place he could see in the best. Are your blinds down?"

"No."

"Well, I'd pull 'em down if I was you." Her voice hesitated a second. "You bein' all alone and all."

"If anybody, Tom or anybody else wants to stand out in

the snow and look in and watch me iron, that's all right with me, Gladys." She made it hearty to put Gladys at ease, it being so new, the word about Royce.

"Oh, Cora." Gladys forced a laugh loud enough to come over the telephone line. Then she said, "Well, I got some more calls to make. I'm down here with the Camerons at the P.O. If you see anything atall suspicious, you give us a ring. A few of the men is out searchin' around camp now."

"Thanks for calling, Gladys."

She pressed down the holder and then put the little black receiver back carefully. She glanced out the window frosted in a white curve near the sill. The moonlight was a shadowed yellow blue on the snow.

Imagine anyone doing something so silly like looking in at people from out in all that cold.

The flatiron had cooled down so it didn't hiss when she touched it with a dampened finger. There was only the sound of the sputtering gas lights. She went back to exchange for one of the heated ones at the back of the stove.

Then she saw him.

A white face almost like it was floating by itself out of the dark at the kitchen window, peering in, the eyes black in the white face watching her. And it was the no expression on the face or in the eyes that was inhuman, terrible, and her breath caught at the back of her throat.

At that instant the face disappeared and she heard voices and feet on the board sidewalk outside.

"There!"

"That's him!"

"Catch him! He's getting away!"

There were running feet, shouts, and she stood with the cold flatiron in her hand by the stove and drew the edges of her sweater together over her thin chest, waiting.

The knock came a few minutes later and it was Les Nickle

panting in great clouds against the dark of the porch.

"We found his footprints right outside your window, Cora. Did you see him?"

"Yes," and he nodded with her like he'd known she had.

"We think we got the bastar– him, but nobody's exactly sure he was the one with the dark and all. Speed asked if you seen him to come over to the office where we're holding him. Get your coat." He blew on his hands, his breath puffing out like smoke. "Lavelle'll be right over to stay in case the kids wake up."

She nodded and went in the bedroom. She heard him stamping off the snow on the porch while she carefully pulled on her pair of shoes, put on her coat and a scarf over her head.

As she closed the front door she could see Lavelle coming across the road, a dark shadow against the snow, half-running that funny way she had. She and Les went down the sidewalk without waiting. The boards had iced over since the snow'd been shovelled off that morning, and Les took her elbow. He had on overshoes with loose clamps that clicked as he walked.

"It's the Willis's nephew who's been up visiting," he said.

All the lights were on in the office, and everyone was standing around watching for her as they came in. Only one man was sitting down in one of the oak office chairs and she looked at him.

He was wearing a khaki uniform with brass buttons that glittered sharply, brilliantly, in the light.

"But he's a soldier."

She found herself shaking as if from cold even though it was warm in the office and someone had turned the gas heater way up.

"Is he the one you seen looking at you, Cora?"

She kept staring at him, his face and his hands the same

whitish color, the long fingers on the wooden arms of the chair. "He's a soldier," she said again.

She could feel Les nodding beside her. "Is he the one?"

She suddenly wanted to hit the expressionless white face with her fist. Smash at the mouth and the nose and feel them give and split and bleed against her hand. He was in the same uniform her Royce had worn with identical brass buttons and olive stripes at the cuffs. He was a soldier, alive and emotionless, looking in at people in lighted rooms, and Royce was dead.

"Yes."

The other men had been waiting tense for her answer and she felt them shift around the chair, relax a little with the certainty.

She wanted someone to strike him, hurt him.

She hadn't taken her eyes off him, and then as she watched, she saw the face alter, crumble sort of, melt. The head moved from side to side, the lids dropped over the black eyes, the nostrils widened, and the lips inverted, skinned back from the teeth as tears eased out onto the cheeks. The upper part of his body shuddered and he cried with his face and his torso while the thin pale hands stayed motionless on the arms of the chair.

She could tell without looking at them that the men didn't know what to do. Out of the corner of her eye she saw one of them walk purposefully over to the telephone. But he didn't pick it up, and everybody stood awkward, grouped, and embarrassed.

Tears splashed down on the khaki jacket, darkened into contained brown dots.

She walked toward the boy.

She felt Les reach out from behind her.

"The poor baby," she said to no one in particular and put out her hand toward the short tow-blond hair.

She touched it and it was like a hairbrush to her palm.

He sobbed forward, sliding from beneath her hand into the front of her coat and his hands left the wood of the chair to clutch at the thick wool of her coat pockets.

She patted his head gently, the scalp pink around the cropped hair.

"The poor baby," she said again.

MERMAIDS SINGING

"IT'S PRETTY STRONG stuff, Mrs. Estes." He looked at her dubiously, holding a fat brown cigarette in each palm. "There's some heroin mixed with the shi—er, a—the grass," he said floundering for a word.

"That's all right, Philip." She lifted it from his hand, careful to keep the ends rolled. It resembled a plump dried tropical fish.

"Okay. If you say so, Mrs. Estes." Then, "Have you got any records? We could use a beat with this."

"There's some stuff Reed left. Over there."

He knelt down and dealt the record jackets out like cards, found one that he carefully arranged on the console. He glanced back at her. "Here," he said coming back quickly. "You hold it like this."

"Are you sure this will smoke?"

"Oh, yes, ma'am."

He brought out a gold Dunhill that seemed so incongruous with the self-rolled dark papered cigarettes that she had to smile.

"Like this?" she said to cover the smile, not to hurt his feelings.

He nodded, intent on steadying the flame against the twisted paper point.

"Cup your hands around it and draw in like you were breathing in steam, or something," he said, briskly lighting his own.

She sucked her breath and the already thick smoke from the dry burning leaves grated the lining of her throat and made her eyes water. She swallowed, reswallowed, trying not to cough.

He sat opposite her, hunched over his own cigarette, inhaling ritually with his eyes shut.

She'd never learned how to inhale ordinary filter cigarettes, and the new harshness searing her throat was unpleasant. But it was her one chance to try it. She knew she could never call and ask him to come again and it was her one chance to see what it was all about, all the things Alec constantly raved over, the new awakening, the new consciousness, freedom, everything Alec said their generation, and particularly she, had missed with their mudfast fifties' morality, her one chance, and she was determined to go through with it.

She drew in hard and held the smoke trapped in her chest.

Philip was leaning back, still inhaling with his eyes shut, cupping the plump dry cigarette with practiced hands. It was amazing how much he resembled her son Reed there in that fireplace chair. It was amazing how much they all looked alike with their hair long to their shoulders like that. She couldn't remember boys in her college days all fading into such a sameness even though they all had short hair, but perhaps it was because these kids were so commonly healthy and all had such straight teeth.

"Feel anything yet?" He was looking at her.

"Not yet."

"How about if we move over to the couch, Mrs. Estes, and I can see up close how you're doing it? You should begin to feel something pretty soon if you're doing it right."

"My name's Laura, Philip." She stood up, aware that she'd almost called him Reed.

"Yes, ma—, uh, Laura."

They sat down on the crushed velvet, close, and he put his own cigarette in the ashtray, placed his hands around hers as he guided the rolled damp paper toward her mouth.

His hands completely covered hers and she looked at them as they came closer to her face. The fingers were long and the nails square, gleaming. It had been a long time since anyone had held her hands, and she felt a vibrating, pulsating in her elbows, temples.

She inhaled obediently, swallowing the smoke.

"Good girl."

He kept his hands on hers for one more drag, then picked up his own. "Just relax and don't think about it. Let it happen."

They smoked silently for what seemed a long time, but when she looked at the cigarette in her fingers, the ash was hardly longer than when she'd sat down.

"Why did you want to do this, Mrs., uh, Laura? Does Mr. E. know?"

"Alec won't be back from his trip until late tonight."

"But why did you want to . . . you know?"

She looked at him, his blue eyes slightly glazed, but serious, intent on her face, and it didn't seem to matter if she told him the truth, it didn't seem to matter how much or what she said.

"He's having an affair with a younger woman."

He nodded.

"His partner's wife. Young, very much . . . ." She couldn't think of the word. ". . . very much attuned," she said finally, "to expression, communication, the idea that sex is just another way of relating to people. She and Alec see each other a couple of times a week and he tells me about their relationship. She's apparently very honest and open, and Alec says that it's only the conventions that are getting in the way of my understanding and enjoyment. He wants me to . . . . They smoke, and . . . well, you know," she finished lamely and took another harsh pull on the cigarette.

He was nodding.

It was the first time she'd said anything to anyone, and it was more difficult than she'd thought. It was hard putting it in words, thick lumped words as heavy as modelling clay, and as she was saying them, she realized she didn't understand at all.

He looked lazily down at his cigarette. "It'd be better if we had a roach clip to get the rest of this, but I guess that's probably enough. It's pretty strong and we don't want to get too much." He seemed to be speaking very softly and slowly. "Too much of anything is too much."

She hadn't noticed before, but looking down she saw the cigarette was short, hot on her fingers. She nodded at him and carefully put the stub in the ashtray, her hand floating free, uncoordinated.

"Okay?"

She nodded and leaned back.

His arm was over the back of the sofa and he touched her hair.

"Alec says they're merely good friends."

"M-m-m-m-m-m."

"He talks about it quite as if it's the most natural thing in the world. But I can't seem to understand. Sex isn't like shaking hands in the street, is it?"

He leaned over her slowly and put his mouth over hers even as she had it open to add another word.

His lips and tongue were moist, suprisingly experienced.

"I—."

"Sh-h-h."

She felt light under him, that he was buoyant above her, their bodies touching and yet not touching as though they were covered by transparent casing, glass sheaths bridging the space between them, her mind filled with swirling reds, oranges, sunflower bursts of magenta. The long hair was strange, awkward, tangling in her hands, womanish, out of place around the male chest that pressed down, away, down, and yet hardly touching her breasts.

Then, what seemed a long time later, she opened her eyes.

The room was still yellow with afternoon sun and his young body lay sleeping across her. Her legs were paralyzed with his weight and she wasn't sure she was breathing.

She saw a long slender strand of dust trailing down from the fireplace mirror.

"Philip." She touched his bare shoulder warm under her palm."

"M-m-m-m-m-m?"

"I can't move."

He opened his eyes and smiled at her.

It had been an equally long time since anyone had opened his eyes and smiled at her.

"I can't move. I'm not sure I can breathe."

"Oh," he said and slid off on his knees to the rug. He leaned back on his heels. "That was good."

She didn't say anything and sat up carefully.

He was watching her. "You still have a nice figure, Laura."

"Thanks a lot."

He grinned. "That was a dumb thing to say."

"That was a dumb thing to say." But she smiled at him.

"I meant it as a compliment."

"I know." She touched his long hair.

"That was great. In waves like the sea. I could almost hear mermaids," he said happily.

A line from Eliot came to her with startling clarity. "I do not think that they will sing to me."

"What?"

"Just something I thought of."

She was suddenly exhausted, drained, inert, tired as she'd never been in her life.

She forced another smile and started picking up the clothes she could reach from where she sat on the couch. He handed her the sweater near him and sat watching her dress.

"You okay?"

"I'm just so tired."

"It does that sometimes the first time."

He stood up and started to tug on his own clothes.

"I'm tired of everything, I think." She pulled the sweater over her head and smoothed her hair. "Of the whole thing. You know, everything."

He nodded. "It sometimes does that, too." He looked down at her. "You focus on things different, see, and you can't really go back to the way things were before."

"Sort of a deus ex marijuana, hm-m?"

"What?"

"Nothing."

He fastened the wide belt and settled it on his hips. His T-shirt had the faded print of a huge violet and orange butterfly. "Laura, would you like to go get a hamburger?"

"Thank you, Philip." She stood up beside him and put her hands on his shoulders, kissed him lightly beside the mouth. "But I don't think so this time."

"I—certainly . . . ."

"Sh-h-h."

He nodded, stood uncertainly for a second, and then, "See you around, I guess."

"Um-m-m-m-m."

He looked back at her from the archway to the hall. "So long."

"Good-bye, Philip."

The front door closed and she leaned against the mantle.

Then she took a deep breath that filled her lungs in two separate syllables and went into the bedroom.

She opened the bureau drawers and laid the stacks of shirts out on the bed. Then the socks, underwear, handkerchiefs, the box of cuff links, tie-tacks he never used, the miscellany that filled his top drawer. From the closet she took out the neat hangers of jackets, slacks, suits, the entire shoe rack, the row of ties, belts.

He was so neat and orderly, so careful that everything matched. His clothes covered the entire king-sized bed. What she couldn't get in his suitcases she'd stuff in cartons from the garage.

"It's twenty years too late, Alec," she said silently, not really needing to say it, already having decided, having reached a conclusion she seemed to have known for months without actually being aware of it, voicing it. "For them it may be real, but for you it isn't, and I've had enough," she said inside her head, moving her lips.

She stood looking down at the bed of suits and shirts and polished shoes. She could hear Philip's young voice saying, "Too much of anything's too much," and she smiled tiredly. She'd have to clear off the bed and put the things on the doorstep before she could lie down.

"It's time for them to sing to me, Alec," she said aloud.

EXILES

THEY SAID IT was the worst weather they'd had in years, the winter I lived in Trieste where the wind peaked the chartreuse waves in the canal beside the Bourse and flung ice from the chartreuse sea against hotel walls that faced the quays. It was a harsh winter and the mail didn't go in or out of Trieste for two months. The wind-battered bricks of the city were always slick, pitted, cold, and I felt a silent, inarticulate sadness hugging the mortar-bound streets, filling the tiny empty park where Italo Svevo stood in iced dark bronze.

I followed the footsteps of James Joyce along the frozen streets, down the alleys of crumbling research, and as I worked, collected, collated in cold damp civic rooms, the dogged and ancient seaport itself became as much an exile for me as the alienated Irishman. The winding streets of the city had allied to no country for very long, had always been

isolated on a jut of land whose neighboring hills belonged to
someone else. The stones of a past owned by everyone, no
one, were piled helter-skelter in the lapidario, age mingling
with age among the trenches down to the new/old Roman
walls. A Roman arch appeared out of a tenement wall, half
swallowed by the plaster, one strut curving out over the
street, the other buried inside the tenement. A great newly
excavated Roman amphitheatre built in the Roman outpost
huddled empty, the wind blowing in from the sea as it had
for centuries.

"You see, the Austrians wouldn't let us dig it out," the
little caretaker of the lapidario said in his precise Italian,
punctuating his sentences with an arm that stopped at the
wrist, his hand lost in a Communist prison after the war, he
explained. "We all knew the amphitheatre was there, but,
you see, they didn't want us to identify with an Italian
heritage. The city belonged to Austria then, and they
wanted us to forget that we were Italian. But everyone
knew it was there." He nodded and thumped the air with his
truncated wrist. "Just as we knew the Roman baths were
here. But we couldn't dig for them until after the war." He
meant World War I.

But somehow the Austrian heritage and the lonely castle
of Miramar jutting out into the sea, a mute reminder of
Maximillian, were as isolated.

"He was very popular with Triestinos," the caretaker
said, a replica of the other little man at the lapidario except
that the casting had included both hands.

"He's a handsome man," I said, looking at the portrait
with its tired green eyes.

"Oh, si, such a handsome man. It was a shame, a sadness,
that his wife insisted they go to Mexico."

And damp with sadness and shame were the stones in the
park of San Giusto. Rough hewn chunks of stone propped

at random on the grass, each painted with a name, a date, sometimes a place, representing a Triestine soldier lost in someone else's war far away from the seaport that Triestinos assured me was fine in summer and only hard in winter.

That winter without mail I moved from whispered bookshelves to unheated archive vaults to boxed papers in empty storerooms, gathering facts and bits of facts about an exiled Irishman in alienated Trieste.

Then one afternoon, an interview was finally arranged with a countess who had known the Joyces personally.

And as I walked toward the apartment high in the center of the hilltop city, it seemed colder than usual, windier, and I pulled my coat tighter around me.

When I reached the number, I went up the wide stairway, around and up to the top floor whose entryway was paved in glittering mosaics as if it were on the ground.

"Buon giorno." A maid bowed me in and the countess came forward, her eyes black in her lined powdered face pale above the black silk dress, the black wool shawl over her shoulders.

"I speak some English," she said. "I learned so many years ago as a girl in school."

She ushered me into a lavish room of ebony, gold leaf, velvet, and her thick coil of silver hair took on the same sheen as the plate beneath luminous silver lamps.

"You would like a scotch and ice, si?" She limped slightly from age and carried a silver tipped black cane. "All my American guests drink scotch and now I never keep another thing for them."

I took the long crystal glass half full of Ballantines and we sat down.

"That's a Renoir, isn't it?" I nodded toward a tiny reclining nude on the wall.

She nodded indifferently. "He was a friend of my father."

She turned to another wall. "That is a much better one by Monet."

"This is a beautiful room."

She sighed. "There were so many things lost in the war. My husband said we should move many things in from the villa, but all of my uncles insisted we were safer out away from the port. My husband brought some of the things in anyway and my uncles smiled at his foolishness." She took a sip from her slender glass of whiskey. "It was not two days later that the American bombers came over and the whole villa was destroyed."

We acknowledged in silence that the Americans and the Italians were accidentally on opposite sides in that war.

"Signore Cagliera told you I was interested in the Joyces?" I said then.

"Oh, si, si." Her gray-white head nodded. "Such a handsome couple. But it was such a shame that they were so ill-matched. She was of the little, the humble, people, and he was an aristocrat in some ways, you know."

By that time, thousands of letters since I'd begun retracing the Joycean past, I'd taken rather a dislike to his selfishness, aristocratic or no, and had taken rather a fancy to Nora, but I merely nodded and listened as she remembered little scenes, little conversations, encounters with the Joyces.

I asked a few questions and she mined her memory until at last she sighed and said, "I suppose this has not been much help to you, but I didn't really know them well. I was their daughter Lucia's age, you know, and they weren't really in our circle." The tall thin crystal cylinder of her glass caught a shaft of light as she took another sip and added, "Poor sad Lucia in that institution all these years, never to have lived at all."

Then her black eyes sent a glitter of light toward me and

she indicated with her silver tipped black cane. "Those are my sons."

I got up to view the photograph of the three laughing young men and I felt her come up beside me.

"Paolo, Vittoria, and Giacomo. That was taken the winter before the war started at Innsbruck where we were skiing. They were twenty-two, twenty, and sixteen then."

They stood laughing in the snow, the sun making black and white shadows on their young faces.

"Paolo and Vittorio went two winters later to the Russian front," she said gazing with me at the silver framed picture.

I didn't say anything. I knew what had happened to the Italians who had marched to Russia with summer uniforms in the winter of 1941.

"Giacomo was too young to go. He was able to stay in school all through the war." She was leaning slightly on her cane. "It was the last week before the Americans came that he and his best school friend persuaded his father that they could help the Partisans hold some Nazis in a building until the Americans arrived. Yugoslavian troops came down from the hills that afternoon. My husband tried to convince them that the Nazis were already trapped and that we had only to wait for the Americans. But the Yugoslavians had not fought much then, you understand, and they insisted that they must kill the Nazis themselves." Her English became slightly more accented, but her tone was the same she had used to talk about the Joyces. "They shelled the building and killed the Nazi's before my husband could stop them. But they killed the Partisans as well."

She turned back to the bottle of Ballantines. "But you must have one small more with me."

As she filled the slender glasses, the scotch splashed the cold warmth of alcohol down my fingers.

"I saw a friend of theirs the other day, one who had been

in school with Paolo. And he was old." Her ancient face smiled. "He had ugly lines and veins and an old bald head, and his jaws had sagged, flabby over his neck. I have my sons young and handsome all."

She gestured again toward the photograph without looking at it. "It is well there is no grave for any of them, my sons. Stones age too, you know, and they are less good to watch grow old."

We drank the scotch and remarked on a Picasso, a small marble Roman Neptune, a medieval Virgin wrought in silver and gold, the oil of her father, the count, who had tried all his life to stop smoking.

When I came down from the mosaic floor of the top of the building, the wind had died down.

I started down the winding street toward the quays, and a block away I could hear the music from the Imperio, music I must have heard, by-passed, a dozen times before.

I paused, watched the twilight blue-green water of the sea, and when I opened the Imperio's door, the lights were yellow, warm, and the voices very loud.

PASCUAS CALEÑAS

I GUESS I must have been about twelve that year. Old
enough to take a taxi to the galeria alone, yet young enough
to accept the urine-soaked sidewalks at the zoo, the front-
page *Tiempo* photos of the latest violencia victims, their
dead eyes staring, the blood from their severed throats black
in print, to accept the beggar on Calle Doce with the great
swollen leg and blue open shin sore, always there with that
gentle half smile on his crumpled face, always there on the
sidewalk by the galeria with his elephantine leg extended.
One of the older girls at school had assured me all beggars
painted their mutilations to attract attention of the gringos,
and I remember looking hard at the sore on the gigantic leg
that seemed ever the same empurpling rotting meat. I stared
at it, but I couldn't tell if he'd touched it up, and even though
I knew better, I dropped a fifty centavo piece in the hat
beside him. He didn't glance up as I stepped over his leg and

passed the squatting fruit vendors, their mounds of chon-
taduras, grapes, lulas, stacked in careful pyramids on brown
fronds or newspapers. Beyond them were the open doors of
the galeria, and I could see the meat hanging in crawling
slabs, the blood slime slushing the floor, the butcher's help-
ers pinching an oozing twist of muscle with beckoning
fingers. I didn't stop for any of them but shook my head and
smiled as they called out, "Venga," "Compre las uvas mas
bonitas, chica," "Venga señorita." It was close to Christmas, the stalls had been set up along Sexta down as far as
Quince, and I had come for them.

Just past the galeria they began, and I walked along
through them, picking, fingering, selecting, haggling because it was no fun for anyone if you didn't bargain, wan-
dering slowly, admiring, receiving my purchases in newspaper cones or palm leaves, and dropping them into the
narrow-mouthed basket on my arm. Even at twelve I knew
enough not to use a wide-mouthed basket. I'd been in the
country long enough for that, especially during the Christmas season.

When I reached Quince I'd have walked back to the
Alferez and home beside the river as I usually did, but I'd
told my mother I'd come by to help her carry things home
from the church. It was the only American church in town,
a composite denominational one with an English service,
and of course the taxi driver didn't know where it was, but
he did nod impatiently at my directions, and we set off,
struggling through the crowds in the center of town, past
the Plaza Caycedo toward Calle Quarta. I looked out the
gritty window at the palms and the string of lights the
American bank had shaped into a Christmas tree, at the men
gathered in the plaza, sitting on benches having their shoes
shined for a peso and having no place to go when the shoes
were finished.

When we got to Calle Quarta I gave the driver added, labored instructions about locating the church, and he nodded, mumbling the house numbers, inching upward until, after only one wrong turning and retracing, he found it.

I gave him his three pesos and lifted my basket onto the grass as he drove off. The heat was stronger there. It slid down from the Everfit deer on the mountain side, past the dry hills, fell in great yellow splotches on the stiff bananas hanging upside down in their tree before the church. I stood there for a minute looking at the hills and the blue mountains beyond the cupped valley, then I went into the church basement where my mother and the other American ladies were working.

They had red and green felt, brought down from the States on somebody's last home leave, spread out over a dozen tables as they busily sewed Christmas stockings and Christmas tree skirts and table covers and little red felt Christmas dresses for little girls who wouldn't be able to wear them because the weather in the valley never changed and Christmas day would be just as hot as every other day. They remembered Christmases from the States that they hoarded, afraid to let go of the things they knew.

I looked at the felt stockings and their designs of wintry sugar plums and snowy stars and I felt somehow sad as though seeing a photograph of myself at five when I was young and round and easily hurt. But I bragged on them when Mrs. Adams asked what I thought, and I helped my mother pack her thin bolts of felt and her packets of sequins for the walk down the hill to our house.

The house smelled like Christmas, a spice smell out of place in the hot noon with the sun falling straight down into the open patio, onto the oranges blooming outside, and I knew the cook had been boiling up the mess my mother insisted would be minced meat for little Christmas pies. Finely chopped fat, two apples flown in especially from

Bogota, cartons of spices and chopped beef, cooked and cooked. But I'd kept tasting it as tin after tin of cinnamon was poured in, and I knew no matter how much my mother's guests exclaimed over the lovely little minced pies, the centers would still be chopped beef hash.

But I didn't say anything that would hurt my mother's feelings. She was always extra-vulnerable around Christmas, and I took my basket into the kitchen, and the maids and I looked at what I'd bought from the stalls before I put the stuff away in my room.

That afternoon after my folks went out again and I was making out my Christmas shopping list on the back of a used memo, the doorbell rang and the maid called up the stairs to tell me Luis was at the door.

I told her to let him in, which she never did unless one of the patronas told her to, and hurried down. I loved Luis's visits. He always dragged in his dirty burlap bag like some mestizo Santa with ragged teeth, and lifted out carefully, almost as if rehearsed, piece by piece, the colonial antiques he sold to gringos. Intricately molded brass and copper estribos used by the Conquistadors, brass bowls and chocolate pots with hammered iron handles, candlesticks, sometimes a colonial painting or an old worm-eaten Spanish missal, but never the same thing twice. I'd become somewhat an authority on colonial work myself from seeing his battered polished metals and from asking him questions about where he found them, and I could spot a phoney or a newly minted estribo the second I saw one.

But that afternoon as I came down the stairs, there was no greasy burlap sack of treasures. There was just Luis standing by the door, not even joking with the maid. He just stood there watching me come down.

"Señorita," he said. He always called me that. "Tengo una problema. Have a problem." He always translated into what English he knew for gringos as if he were afraid we wouldn't understand, but his English was pretty bad. "Mi hija está muerta y necessito cincuenta pesos por la sabana." And he didn't translate that part. As though the death of his daughter and his begging for fifty pesos was too painful to put into a second tongue, as if it couldn't be said more than once.

I hesitated. Death in the family or an unexpected illness of somebody you never heard of was the standard excuse of the servants when they wanted off or wanted extra money to go on a holiday to Tumaco. And usually we didn't see them again; some relative came to pick up their things and that was that. And here was Luis not even employed in the house. We saw him only every few weeks as it was. He watched me hesitating and his red-rimmed eyes dropped.

I guess that did it. The red rims of his eyes dropping before mine.

I knew better, but I said, "Momento," and went back upstairs. I had some money of my own from allowances and birthdays, and I rummaged in the little locked wooden box, counting out enough to make fifty pesos.

Like I say, I knew better, but I took it down anyway, and gave it to him.

"Gracias, señorita," he said and disappeared outside again.

The maid didn't say anything, just shook her head as I went back to my room again.

That night at dinner when I told my folks, my father said, "Well, that's fifty pesos you'll never see again." And they both agreed that it was just as well I'd learned that lesson with my own money.

I moped around, kicking myself for wasting fifty pesos that could buy a lot then, and as the household got ready for Christmas, I got sicker about my money. I'd been in the country longer than that. And yet I'd given my money away. I'd fallen for the oldest gimmick in the city. I'd been gulled out of almost my entire savings.

We already had our Christmas tree up at home, set up in the living room, raining pine needles on the marble floors. I'd wanted one of those stripped branch trees the Colombians use, but my folks insisted on the traditional green American kind, as if Christmas wouldn't be the same without the fir and the balls imported from the States and all the icicles that the gringos carefully picked off their trees and left with some chosen friend when they went home for good. I looked at the tree and felt awful about my money.

The next day was no better, and the closer it got to Christmas, the worse I felt.

I borrowed money on my allowance that put me in hock up until the middle of February to buy expensive handmades at the American church bazaar instead of going to the stalls downtown. I felt the vendors in the streets could see I was a mark, and that they set their prices accordingly. I couldn't bargain without suspicion, and the joy I'd felt in walking among the stalls had dissolved.

I knew I was taking it too hard, but I had really liked Luis and the things he brought, and I liked to hear him tell about the Spanish and the colonies. After that he couldn't dare come back to our house of course. The story about his dead daughter was too apt, too pat to have happened just before the Christmas season. Probably fifty pesos worth of that licorice tasting aguardiente was what I'd bought, not the winding sheet and wooden coffin for a funeral. I felt used and bitter.

Then on Christmas Eve as my folks were getting ready to go out to an early cocktail party, of which there were always plenty among the gringos for any holiday, the doorbell rang.

"If that is the garbage men for their Christmas bonus, I have some loose pesos in the box on my desk," my mother called from her bedroom in that stiff voice she used while arching her eyelids for mascara. "Six or eight will be enough depending on how many there are."

"Okay."

I scooped them up and went to the stairs. "Quien es, Florinda?"

She came to the stairs with a newspaper wrapped parcel. "Para usted," she said and held it up to me.

"Que es?"

"No se." She shrugged and gave it to me.

It wasn't very heavy, wadded in newspaper and tied around the middle with a dirty fraying rope.

I poked at its lumpiness as I went to my room and laid it on the bed.

"Was that the garbage men, dear?"

"Nope." I slipped off the rope and the newspaper fell open. A carved, painted, wooden baby in a filthy velvet robe lay inside. The baby was holding up two wooden fingers toward me and gazing at me with blue glass eyes. The pink had worn off slightly from the carved fingers and toes, and the gilt had chipped from the edging golden curls around the face, but otherwise the figure was in perfect condition. I recognized it immediately. A wooden eighteenth century quiteño statue. A goldleafed, colonial Baby Jesus in aged red velvet.

An envelope lay under the baby, and I took it out. "Para la señorita," it read on the outside, and as I opened it, a cheap communion card printed with a fuzzy Madonna and child fell out. "Felices Pascuas" was written in pencil across the back and the name "Luis Ortigas" was carefully signed underneath.

He had brought me a Christ child on Christmas Eve, worth a dozen times the fifty pesos he didn't have in cash. I sat down on the bed with the little card in my hand. The little painted face of the baby looked calmly up at me.

INDIAN BURIAL

NOBODY KNEW ABOUT her spot and she sure as hell wasn't going to tell them.

She hitched up a shoulder to scratch the small of her back and took out a cigarette. She held the steering wheel with one hand, tamped the cigarette to let the bits of tobacco flake loose out on the dashboard.

That prissy Lena with her flowery pack, some silly woman filter to show off dainty and let some man light it for her. What the hell kind of smoke is that? She touched the red circles of the lighter to her Camel.

Men're so damned stupid. Weak and stupid, the lot of them.

She ought to know. Married four times with five kids, twins with that namby pamby Willis, and who'd think he'd even have one kid let alone two at once. Four husbands and not one of them worth the powder to blow him to hell.

Twenty-three lovers besides, or was it twenty-four, she always had to stop and count if she wanted it exact and "lovers" certainly wasn't the word anyway, not a one of them worth a damn.

In all those years if she'd just found one, even one, that'd given her anything. Anything at all besides some accident that'd come bursting out nine months later leaving her with another squalling brat just when she was getting the others so they could take care of themselves.

But she had to hand it to Matt. He'd had sense enough to take off on his own without waiting to have her throw him out, locking the door and chucking his shoes out a window the way she'd done with all the others when she was sick of them drinking up her restaurant money.

She ground out the half-smoked cigarette, feeling the damp tip where her lips had been. No matter how hard she tried, she never could keep from wetting the paper, and then the clammy end in her mouth always ruined the smoke.

Maybe she ought to get one of those holders with a plastic mouthpiece after all. Matt suggested her getting one once but she'd just sneered at him, having better things than that kind of damn nonsense to spend her money on. She'd kind of hoped he'd get one anyway, let her know it was a gift, let her know he was boss, but he didn't. And a couple of years later he was gone, taking Sammy with him.

She'd never understood that. Sammy wasn't even his own kid but belonged to that lazy Manuel who was her husband the shortest of all and who she was never sure why she married in the first place except that she was angling for his brother Raul and he'd got in the way. And Sammy was certainly no damned bargain with all that dark skin and her blue eyes, but wishy washy like, staring off into space, floating like loose marbles in his head if she ever shouted loud enough to get his attention. Always fiddling with a pencil or a crayon or some damn thing, one time even drawing up a whole pad she needed for taking down orders. That was the one time she'd seen Matt mad, violent mad, pushing her off from Sammy, jerking away the belt she was beating him with, yelling at her not to touch the kid. He even tossed a couple of dollars on the floor to pay for "the fucking paper." She remembered it exactly, his angry voice using a word she always made clear no one was to use in her presence.

"Oh what the hell." No use spoiling the day.

It wasn't often any more she got away from the restaurant what with not being able to afford much help and trying to stay open as much as possible. It was funny how with the country getting prosperous again that the food and motel business had gone off so. Of course Flagstaff wasn't what it once was with big chain motels moving in and all. She didn't ask questions when somebody checked in for a couple of hours at the full night's rate, but you still had to change the sheets after, wearing them out with washing.

Well, no use thinking about that either.

Here she'd got the afternoon away and that was what she ought to be thinking about. Getting to the spot no one knew about, digging out in the sun, letting the heat warm her clear through, maybe making that big find she could sell to the museum in Tucson. Matt was good for that at least, getting her onto the digging for Indian treasure. No use thinking about the other crap.

A dense flight of orange butterflies rose ahead, hundreds of them filling the sky, the highway ahead of her, catching in the air currents as the car overtook them, smashing out of control on the windshield, leaving yellow blotches of insect entrails over the glass.

"Goddamn nuisances." It was hard enough to see with the damned glare on the hood and the blacktop without all that mess.

She peered through the yellow-white scum. The car kept

hitting into them even as they tried floating, flying out of the way, hundreds more of them.

And the dirt road was along there somewhere. She had to slow down.

There it was.

She turned sharply off the highway onto the road that was hardly more than a wagon path, and great banks of dust rose immediately on each side of the car.

She was forced to slow down even more, guiding the car in ragged tracks hard and stiff as concrete.

Past the first crop of foothills in a little valley sort of place was where it was, where she'd found all the arrowheads that last time.

She kept her eyes half on the rise of the hills, half on the ruts, looking hard through the dirtied windshield, and she was suddenly jolted to see a man beside the road.

She got closer and saw it was an old Indian, hair lank and dirty-looking below a round-brimmed gray hat, shoulders stooped in a greasy jacket too big for him.

As she drove slowly past she saw him dig in the little brown dime store sack he carried, extract a red candy ball and put it carefully in his puckered mouth.

"Old fool." She glanced back at him from the rear-view mirror. Standing out there in the middle of nowhere sucking ten cent hard candy. "Probably not a tooth in his head."

But then as she got to the row of foothills she forgot about him. It was right along there, and she had a feeling about her luck that afternoon.

She drove through and got to a spot she thought she recognized, the sagebrush looking right. She stopped, stared at it until she was almost sure, and turned off the motor.

No use pulling off the ruts and risking getting stuck in that soft looking dirt when nobody'd be coming by anyway.

She jammed a sweat stained hat down on her head and got out the shovel and trowel.

Matt'd been good for something anyway. More than the rest of them.

She walked out from the car to where she was sure she'd found the points that last time. A rain had eroded down the side of what looked like a mound and she stooped to look at the gouge in the dry earth.

Sure enough. There were two pot sherds sticking straight out of the water cut. Red clay pieces about the size of quarters but there they were all right. It was the place.

She put down the trowel and started digging in the side of the little hillock. Slow, careful, methodical, watching sharp-eyed each shovelful as it was pulled out of the earth and dumped to the side. Whenever she saw a sherd or a chip of flint or a shred of bone, she stopped, picked it out, and put it aside. At least half a dozen different bowls or pieces of them were in the mound.

Sweat collected under the hat brim, on her upper lip, ran down her backbone and down the crease between her breasts. She always felt like taking off the heavy drill shirt and digging in her bra, but she never did. Matt'd've liked that. All they ever thought about was sex.

To hell with them.

The pile of dirt grew as her shovel dug, lifted, emptied.

Then it happened.

The way Matt described it might when he'd got her interested in hunting for Indian burials in the first place.

The shovel struck rock where there should've been only dry loam. She tossed the shovel down and started with the trowel, scraping off the dirt to expose flat stones laid carefully over something the Indians wanted to protect.

She worked steadily, carefully, laying bare the stones that fitted together like a flagstone walk.

She'd cleared a space about four feet long when the stones ran out.

It was too damned small. She couldn't remember if they were supposed to have flexed burials or not.

Maybe it wasn't a burial after all.

She dug some more, but that was all of it. Only four feet. The end stones went down, encasing, enclosing whatever it was in a stone box.

That's the way it always happened. Just when she had something good going, it all went to hell.

She got down on her knees and started lifting the rocks off the top, afraid she might drag away some and the rest'd fall in and crush the treasure, if there was one. But as she worked she could see the hole had already filled with dirt and she could lift the stones off without worrying.

She started with the trowel again, the sweat running down from her hat to her eyebrows, and she wiped it off with her sleeve. Her tongue felt swollen, dry as the earth as she heaped it out.

She didn't stop to examine any more, just watched as the dirt was lifted out by the trowel.

"Damn."

It was a burial after all.

Not of somebody flexed, but of a kid.

From the size of the skull and the teeth she could see coming out of the dirt, it'd probably been about two years old.

She leaned back on her heels.

Little bone hands lay at the sides of the rib cage filled with dirt. Beside the head was a buff colored bowl and some rough beads curved like they'd been strung on a thread long since rotted away.

She dug carefully again until at last she had it all exposed, the little skeleton, the bowl, the flat stones of the grave floor.

Her hands rested on her knees and she looked down at them. Dirt stuck to them in random patches and the enlarged blue veins at the backs protruded in great ugly ridges. Her hands were old, old like the rest of her, dry and crackled.

She could feel the back of her boots against her thighs.

Out there all alone it wasn't enough, wasn't anything. That old fool Indian in the middle of nowhere sucking hard red candy.

A movement caught her eye and she looked up from the grave.

The mass migration of orange butterflies had reached where she was. They filled the air above her in a thick orange cloud, fluttering like burnt-orange ashes, sifting, glittering stained glass wings hazing against the sun.

"God damn you," she said softly. "God damn you to hell."

THE CAKE EATERS

IT WOULD HAVE been a good day to dance naked on the balcony, the rain like a silvered veil around her and her body undulating, glistening, becoming a liquid rhythm above the street, flowing with the rain, her hips that Dave said were too fleshy melting into the fine mist.

But they'd be there any minute and she put another green line above her lashes instead.

Then she got out the embroidered napkins she'd bought that time she chaperoned the senior class to Miami where they had so many little treasures like that in the airport. They'd notice of course that she didn't have any flowers in the center of the table since the heat had charred the last pot of her geraniums, but this time they could very well appreciate the napkins she'd never used before and the beautiful cake.

It was beautiful, flawless, the most perfect cake she'd ever made, and she stood admiring it against the background of the fine rain outside the balcony, lost in the creamy pink and white beauty of it. And when the bell rang, she jumped, a startled catch in her throat.

"Yoo-hoo, Alma."

It was Nick and Peter and Peter had on his Petit Ecole gym instructor sweat shirt that he thought showed off his biceps. As they came in Peter said, "O-o-o-o-ey. It's raining cats and dogs out here," and shook out the umbrella he carried for the two of them.

Nick smiled fondly at him and Alma wondered how he managed that smile every time, especially since he knew Peter picked up soldiers from Biloxi every time he went off to visit his mother in Hattiesburg.

They went toward the French doors where she'd set up the table.

"Did you make that, Alma Pettifore?"

"O-o-o-o-ey, look at that."

She nodded, knowing Peter was just a bit envious since he hadn't the decorator's knack she did and always had to leave his cakes plain iced. "It's two boxes of angel food and some extra egg whites. I think an angel food cake should be high."

"Alma certainly has the right name, eh, Nick?" Peter reached back and Nick took his hand and squeezed it.

She'd told them how Dave had kidded her about her name every time she'd made him a cake, and how he'd laughed and said she did have the soul of a little cake.

"I can pig myself on angel food with roses like this once in a while, but there's something about a chocolate cake with that thick icing you make," Nick said diplomatically.

"I'll put on the water for tea," she said quickly. Sometimes Nick was just too much. Peter did have a nice body, but surely even Nick could see he had a brain the size of a red bean.

"Is Louise coming this afternoon?" They settled in two chairs side by side.

"She's coming, but she has to pass the Red Rocker, and you know what an antique nut she is."

Peter giggled. "Especially with Wilted Walter's money."

Alma filled the copper teakettle.

"Oh, guess who we saw in the Jersey Lily the other night?" Nick said and put his arm beside Peter's. They both had on thick wristlets of leather.

"Who?"

"Guess."

"I can't think who it'd be. The drinks are too expensive in there."

"Oh, guess." Nick looked as if he might pout, but Peter took his hand and said, "Dave," before he had a chance to.

"Dave?" She tried to say it the same way he had, bright and quick and as if it was just a name like anybody's name. But there was a thud inside her, a jolt as if she'd stepped off a bus and missed the last step, and she knew what it'd be like if she saw him, even though she'd prepared herself in case she ever ran into him around town. She'd told them all that Dave had been a beautiful experience and who cared if it didn't end in marriage, but even as she'd said it, she knew she'd have done anything to have him marry her, anything, and she felt they knew it too, that everyone knew it right after she walked in that time and his clothes were gone from the closet, his shaving things from the bathroom cabinet, his towels that had so mingled with hers over the year that she hadn't remembered which were his until she saw them missing from the shelf.

"Dave?" She tried it again to get the casual tone right, but it still wasn't. The apartment was so empty without him, his ties, his smell. "I hope he was spending piles of his money, the cheapskate."

"You know how expensive the Jersey Lily is," Nick said, echoing her and she sensed he was kindly not telling her that Dave was with a girl, and it was all right as long as he didn't tell her and she didn't know for sure.

The teakettle whistled shrilly, and she could say from the kitchen alcove, her back to them, "Sometimes I'm not sure that Dave didn't like guys better than girls anyway." She gave a little laugh.

Peter giggled with her. "I wondered about that sometimes myself."

But he said it too quickly and she knew he never had, that he was being kind, and she had to blink suddenly to bring the china teapot back into focus as she poured in the boiling water.

She waited a second, then carried it to the table, able to face them and smile without a tremor. "I hope Louise will be here by the time that steeps."

If Louise was too late they could start on the tea, but she wouldn't let them spoil the cake before everyone saw it.

But even as she was trying to find something else to add, something else to say to their waiting faces, the bell rang.

"I wonder what she bought today," Peter said.

"With Wilted Walter's money," Nick added softly as Alma went to the door to let her in.

Louise came in with a brown paper package that was an awkward wrinkled sack. "Wait till you see this." She breezed straight for the table, talking with quick words through her passage. "It's one of those Victorian pieces I just can't resist. And they were only asking eight dollars for it." Her voice went on breathlessly as she took it out of the sack and set it on the table, a bronze Leda with a dusty tarnished swan biting his wing while metal vines and cracked, chipped crystal leaves entwined them both.

"Isn't that lovely." She was talking breathlessly, panting

from the climb up the stairs, but there was something not right in her tone that Alma couldn't put her finger on.

"When it's polished up it can really be a pretty thing." Alma tried to peer at it appreciatively, but it was hideous and filthy beside her beautiful cake.

"How do they make that kind of thing?" Nick reached out and touched it gingerly.

"They don't make them any more. It's an antique."

"Don't be bitchy, dear," he smiled at her.

"We don't want the tea to get too strong. Why not sit over there, Louise."

They sat down and pulled the chairs closer to the table.

"Have you seen Carlos lately?"

"Oh, yes. This morning in fact." Louise's eyes glittered strangely.

Alma decided instantly that must be it. They all knew Louise had been having an affair with her Cuban doctor, one of those who flocked to the coast after Castro and was somehow able to get licensed. Something must have gone wrong between them. There wasn't any future in it anyway with his wife and that herd of Catholic children they had.

"Now we can cut the cake," Peter said. "I'm starved."

Alma felt he almost wanted to cut it just to destroy it.

"Do you want to do it?"

He looked at her and seemed to know what she was thinking. "It's your creation, sweety."

She took her grandmother's lovely old cake knife with the pearl handle and carefully sawed down into the icing, through the spring of the angel food.

"Isn't it lovely?" Louise said, her eyes glittering.

Alma cut great slices, trying to preserve as much of each rose as she could, and passed them around. They sat motionless in deference to the cake while she poured the tea in the thin cups. Then they pressed their forks in unison into the fluffy trapezoids of cake.

"M-m-m-m-m-m."

"Delicious."

They ate in silence and sipped their tea quietly.

"That was great."

Alma glanced up. Louise sat with her back to the window and the pots of wilted geraniums, her mouth full of cake, bits of frosting dotting her lipstick, and tears running down her cheeks.

"For heaven's sake, what's the matter?"

Louise shook her head and the tears sprayed off, splattered somewhere on the table.

"What is it?" Nick said putting down his fork beside his plate.

"It's just . . . ." The cake and icing coated, blurred the words, showed thick and pink wet around her teeth.

They all sat and looked at Louise whose eye make-up had begun to dribble into the tears that spilled out in rapid drops.

At last Louise swallowed the cake.

"I have a brain tumor," she said.

"What?"

"A brain tumor." She said it again, louder and wiped her face with the embroidered napkin, smearing a stubby steak of black across it. "Carlos got the report and told me this morning."

Alma couldn't think of anything to say. She glanced at Nick and Peter across the table, but they were both staring at Louise.

Then Nick recollected himself. "That's heavy."

"O-o-o-o-ey." Peter shook his head.

There was a silence and a car honked on the street below and a shrill voice cut through the steady drip of rain on the balcony.

Louise looked at each of them in the face, her eyes wide and wet, and then she smiled a wavering smile.

Alma took a shallow breath that didn't seem to get to her lungs at all. She sliced through the fat pink roses as she cut another wedge of cake for each plate.

There was a click of polished silver forks against the china as they leaned forward and began to eat.

BULLFIGHT

1

THE SUN WEIGHED down on her, filling her pores, coating her forehead, her eyelids as the procession began and the rhinestone crusts of the suits bored into her eyes. The day seemed hotter, more crowded than last year. Nothing was the same as last year, would ever be the same. She glanced away from the arena, down at her program, and she didn't know any of the bullfighters, wasn't sure she wanted to spend three more days at the corridas now that it had been said aloud in the tired hotel room. The bloated wine skin pressed against her ribs, a swollen growth under her arm as the crowd swayed.

Fat white doves rose in nervous flight, awkward white wings flapping past the upper tiers, the city flags, toward the hooded mountain of the Sleeping Lady. Sleeping the way I've been, she thought, not wanting to know, pretending, and yet knowing even asleep. She passed Charles the wine skin, and his gold wedding ring glinted thickly in the sunlight.

Rain-worn gates swung back and the bull hurtled onto the sand. She was conscious of the silver sparks from the goad, horns like burnished ornaments. The matador, a satin allegory of courage against darkness, stood a jewel encrusted phallus against the panting, heaving blackness of the evil.

She watched the cape tease the rubbed horns, whip aside to curl like an affectionate pet around the satin body. Pink ankles balanced immobile as hooves pounded beside them. The large pink cape lashed against its own gold side again and again, flicking, avoiding the horns, and she took the moist wine skin and pressed it above her mouth, the green crystalline wine spraying down her throat, leaving an aftertaste on her teeth.

The metallic cry of the trumpet shattered the hypnotic pink-gold swirl of canvas, and the wing of cloth drooped, rested against the sand.

A padded, blindfolded horse trod lightly, carefully, feeling the way with graceful pawing legs. Sun arched from the steel legging, the barber-pan helmet, the perforated mitten of the picador. The blinded horse's head tossed in the unseen sun as the great horns crashed into the padding and the thick metal point gouged, dug into the quivering back, a knife in live vibrating muscle on a counter top, gouged again, until through the sieve of the sun, the trumpet called once more.

A steady crimson flow layered, matted the fur. The now scarlet cape, hovering, dodging, hovering again over the horns, damped into black as it fondled the bloodied sides.

At last the scarlet cape dragged against the sand, and the lolling tongue of the bull hung toward it. Sparkling youth and wounded evil stood blankly poised before the blade glinted over the horns and slipped between the shoulder blades. The bull waited unaware, the monstrous tongue hanging. Then the front legs fell in like pressed straws, a jet of urine and a thick rope of blood appeared at the same instant and the massive body collapsed.

Dark evil succumbed once more to jeweled bravery. The satin emblem of courage raised shimmering arms and bloodied cape, and she passed the wine back to Charles. Three days more and he'd go back to his wife, back for good to the correct and victorious legend of his married life.

White handkerchiefs of approval began to flutter in the rows around her. Charles shook out his monogrammed, blue-edged one, and smiled at her as he waved it too.

A brace of bell-jangling mules dragged the dead bull across the arena, leaving a wide sweep of brushed sand and blood, the trumpet called, brass-throated, and the ritual began again in new shouldered, horned blackness, flowing amber ribbons, a fresh pink-gold cape, a second matador in white satin and gold. The polished horns were even wider, bent uneven, and once more the picador jabbed the quivering live meat, unbloodied banderillas pierced the fur to prepare for the clean red cape.

She watched, tasting another arc of wine that made her want to touch Charles and yet want not to, knowing her fingertips already superfluous. The gold-white man furled and unfurled the cape at the crooked horns.

Then it was time for the kill once more, and she saw the momentary pause, the lunge.

The gleaming horn lifted, hooked into the satin groin.

The white satin body raised stiffly on the horn, then dropped, splashed with a great blossom of red. She felt the wine skin on her lap, and the crimson stain on the white satin crushed through a fragile partition in her quivering mind. She knew suddenly that this was what she'd waited for. Not consciously wanting, yet secretly hoping for, waiting for, exulting in. A body flung up by a horn that gouged deep in the flesh beneath the satin, a body thudding onto the sand. The justification of evil, triumph of adultery, sin, and the perversion of the myth.

2

The sand of the arena was a good dry grit. He analyzed it with his soles as he strode beside Puerto in the procession. It was good sand for capework. Puerto and his luck with the draw had won the first bull of the afternoon, and he would follow Puerto's careful kill. The Andalusian peasant was nothing in capework, but the crowd always forgot a careless muleta in the face of a good kill.

Sweat was at his eyebrows by the time they bowed to the judges. He leaned on the wood railing with the capote over his arm and watched them release the doves. He gazed up at the crowd. They swayed like seed grass, and he looked at them and knew what would please them, what would turn them into a wave of fluttering handkerchiefs, shouting to present him an ear.

The first bull was an azabache, black, 440 kilos. It thumped the earth with spirit, tried to loosen the goad in its back. With Puerto's usual luck it was a fine bull with balanced corniapertado horns and head held low.

The capote work was merely adequate. Puerto stamped like a picador's horse, took sips of water that he rolled in his mouth, spat into flowers of beaded dust at his feet.

The muleta was hardly better. Simple half veronicas, naturals, stiff and ungraceful. Puerto worked close to the tablas.

But Puerto lowered the muleta, aimed between the balanced horns in the moment of truth, and the sun, seconds before eclipsed by a cloud, poured over the azabache luster of the bull, over the suit of light. Puerto and the bull posed in the brilliance before Puerto lunged. His blade slid between the vertebrae as though plunged in loose sand. The bull twisted its head from side to side. The steel cut through veins, arteries, aorta, and the bull dropped. It was a clean, quick kill.

The white kerchiefs began even before the mono sprang forward to jab the knife behind the bull's head. Puerto looked up smiling, his palms held wide over his head, teeth chalked across his face. The Presidente nodded, and Puerto got the ear. An ear merely for a kill. He would show them what could be done with a muleta.

His was a 395 kilo bull named Arco Azul. But as it pounded from the gate, he could see the wide curved horns, the left dipping low with spear-point sharpness. A bizco. The animal tossed its head, carved the air with the uneven horns. He stepped out, not waiting for Enrique to make the preliminary passes, whirled the capote into a veronica. The bull saw him at once and charged, head up, and the low left horn caught, almost jerked the cape from his hands as it ripped through the layers of cloth.

He studied the bull after the picador, the banderilleros had finished. The head was still too high. The kill would be an awkward one. He took the muleta and shook it out in the tercio. A breeze caught the cloth, and the bull charged, lifting the spear horns as it passed. He signalled for water on the muleta, dragging it in the dust to muddy it against the wind. And the cape obeyed him, not the wind, as he passed the bull again and again.

He nodded for the curved sword of the kill, poised between the crooked horns, and aimed for the recess between the shoulder blades.

Too late he saw the head jerk up, close the space between

the bones. Too late he saw the wet eyes of the bull, the horns twist as he was pushed to meet them. He felt himself lifted from the ground and the scarlet muleta fold around him. He saw gold churned earth, black sodden fur, and then the black mosaic squares filling in from the edges of his sight.

3

But the other bullfighter, the first one, came back into the arena, came back to finish the bull with the crooked horns, and she watched the scarlet cape, the tapering, glittering sword return to right the myth.

WROUGHT IRON LACE

I TOOK TO him right off.

The minute he walked in with Mrs. Larimore I took to him.

It'd started out one of those shitty parties where you want to be somewhere else, not any place else special, you know, but just away. Not that everything wasn't all right with the way it was going, smoke from the hash and incense lacing back and forth like ribbons in the black light, everybody with it, swaying, dancing, but it was that the pad was, well, Jim's pad and he'd brought me up once, just the two of us. It'd been my first, but of course I didn't tell him that, and I suppose everyone remembers her first more than anything, even though Carla said she'd heard that once you've had a dozen or so, you can't even recall that first one's name. But that was part of it, I guess, the party being there at Jim's.

Of course I was getting enough attention even without

Jim. Harold with his crazy—and I mean really crazy like they had him down at the psychiatric ward for observation after he'd demanded a Ph.D. from Tulane because Dr. Stimson had one and he, Harold, certainly knew more than old Stimson—hungry eyes was giving me the big silent rush, and I'd about decided to go back to his place with him.

I can dig Afros after a couple of drags, and I was beginning to think what the hell, you should have a black these days anyway. Carla says you're really out of it if you've never tried one, and certainly it'll show Jim what I think of him, that I certainly don't give a damn if he never called, or calls, me again. Everyone would know about it by the next day, of course, and it'd serve him right to have me walk out of his place with a black, and I'd almost decided.

But then they came in.

There were the three of them together, Dr. Whitson in a suit and tie like the fifties, stiff and yet soft at the same time in a sort of hard stale eclair sort of way, and Mrs. Larimore in a black dress of some kind with gold jewelry you could tell even across the room was real. And then him.

Probably nobody but me noticed him right away because Dr. Whitson and Mrs. Larimore are pretty popular and it was as if they were somehow spotlighted, almost, bringing their own light with them, you know, with Dr. Whitson's red glowing pipe and those dabs of gold jewelry on her. And he kind of stood there with them, outside their light, uncomfortable and alone.

Mrs. Larimore was introducing him around as the kids kind of crowded up, but casual, so no one'd think they were sucking up to a prof, and I watched him standing there vulnerable and at the same time sort of bearlike, and I made up my mind to go home with him whoever he was.

I could see by the way he wasn't touching Mrs. Larimore or even looking at her that he was wanting to, but I could tell by the casual way she was smiling and saying his name to the kids around that she wasn't that interested somehow. I suppose maybe that's something every woman knows about another, when they want some guy and when they don't, and I knew for whatever reason she didn't. Not that *that* would've mattered of course since she must be forty or so and you know how skin gets kind of like crepe then no matter how good a care you've taken of yourself.

I waited for the crowd to thin out some and then I patted Harold on his stiff black hair. "Be right back," I said loud in his ear so he could hear over the music, feeling the cartilage against my lips as I moved them. He looked at me and I knew he knew I wasn't coming back at all.

But he grinned that crazy grin with his narrow mouth that's more like a white man's than a black's mouth and said, "See you, baby."

I shoved my way through the dancers, but still casual, and got over to them.

"Hi," I said.

Mrs. Larimore smiled. "Saranell Birdsong," she said, "Ben Random, the famous author."

He glanced at her quick without meaning to and then back at me and I could tell her saying that after his name hurt him even though I couldn't see why it should have.

Then he grinned at me and said, "That's some name."

"It's an old New Orleans name," I said, giving him the wide blues. "My gran'mere had the exact same name when she lived on Royal Street at the turn of the century."

He was looking at the shrink I had tied with just a couple of thongs, and I moved a little to let him see I wasn't wearing anything under it. Any man goes for that kind of thing, and I knew I could get his attention any time I wanted to.

"Did you and Dr. Whitson get a drink, Mrs. Larimore?" I

said and let him have my profile that Jim said really seriously ought to make a cameo. I turned so he could see down the shrink and my skin tanned all the way down to my hip huggers.

"Let me get you all something," Jim popped up from somewhere, and Larry beside him nodded as if he'd said it.

I didn't look at Jim any more than if he'd been anybody who was having a party. That Larry with his long silky hair all over the place, always hanging around Jim. Maybe that could explain why Jim never called me back.

"Nothing for me right now," the one named Ben Random said like he wasn't sure whether Jim really was talking about all of them. "That hard stuff is too much for me."

I thought maybe he was saying he'd rather have a whiff of grass or something rather than a mixed drink to let us all know he was really with it.

"Are you really a famous author?"

He grinned lopsidedly, looking at me but not missing that Mrs. Larimore and Dr. Whitson were going off with Jim and Larry. I pretended I was too engrossed with him to notice how Jim was striding off in those tight jeans. "I guess that depends on your definition of 'famous.' "

"But you are an author? And you don't work, you just write books."

He laughed. "That's safe to admit, I guess. I don't work, I just write books."

"I've never known anyone like that."

"Well, Saranell Birdsong, whose grandmother had the exact same name, you know one now."

The way he said it made my breath and my muscles sort of quiver somewhere at the top of my stomach.

"Would you like to see the balcony? The French Quarter always looks better from somebody's balcony."

He made a funny sort of bow with his hand out and I led
the way to one of the French windows that led outside. I
went right through the middle of the dancers with him
trailing me so everybody'd see I had him as soon as he came
in.

There were a couple of other people outside, but off in the
dark corner and I led him over to the railing.

"Isn't this a swell night?" It was cool and clear and not
even a hint of that usual New Orleans rain in the air.

"I didn't know anyone used that word anymore," he said
and looked out over the balcony.

"What?"

"Nothing."

He stared at the wrought iron grill on the balcony opposite that was like dust webs in the streetlamp light.

"Isn't this nice?"

"H-m-m-m-m-m."

He looked down at the street then, his hands on the
railing, kind of leaning over a little, and I got the funniest
feeling he wanted to jump, you know like when you watch
a line of traffic coming at you when you're crossing Canal
Street and you have the weirdest urge to step out in front of
it. But he didn't move, he just leaned and looked down.

I hadn't noticed inside, but out in the night with just the
street light, I saw he was growing a beard. A wayout little
beard, kind of light blond and silk furry just on the point of
his chin. It was funny looking and yet kind of sad that he
couldn't grow a really good one.

The silence was getting too long even with the music so
loud inside, and I thought about saying all the things you
say like asking him if it was the first time he'd been in New
Orleans, or if he liked the South, or liked to travel when he
wrote, or any of the stuff you're supposed to say to get

acquainted with, but I watched him look up and study that fleecy wrought iron across the way like it was going to move.

"Are you and Mrs. Larimore having an affair?" I said instead.

I think he might have started a little if he hadn't been braced on the balcony rail, but he looked at me cool as if he wouldn't have, and wouldn't have been surprised at anything anyway. "Would you divorce your husband for me, Saranell Birdsong?"

"I don't even have a husband." I wanted to giggle.

He looked away again, up at the rooftop and the sky that had lots of stars. "Did you know we can get caught in the rules of rebellion as easy as in the conventions of conformity."

He wasn't really talking to me and it wasn't making much sense. I'd already decided I was going to go to bed with him, so I didn't need to listen too well.

My figure beat out anybody's at that party, and while Mrs. Larimore might be cool and distant and he might've been looking at her, good grief, she was certainly no beauty.

I laughed a little, my throaty Cher laugh, to get him out of that talking to himself mood and back to me. I took a deep breath and said, "You want to fuck me?"

He glanced at me. "Why not?" he said.

I don't think most guys would've reacted that way, and I'm sure that's not what they usually say.

I wondered what you were supposed to do then. I could feel my heart pounding fast, almost jumping out of the shrink. But he didn't seem to notice and was looking back at the sky.

"And you find out there's nothing out there when you're alone, nobody to talk to who can understand . . . anything . . . ." He looked back at me a second. "You've picked a worn out, tired old man, honey."

"How old are you for pity's sake?"

He didn't answer, he just kept looking at me or sort of through me really, and then he said slowly, "Shaw once said it's just as well the young don't know what the forty-year-olds are thinking."

"That's a funny thing to say."

"Yeah, isn't it?" But I could tell he didn't think it was any funnier than I did.

And then all of a sudden, he took my hand, sort of sighed, and pulled me along side of him back into the party.

He looked around for a second adjusting his eyes to the dark and then went straight over to Mrs. Larimore.

"Saranell and I are going to split, Jo," he said, looking at her a long look, wanting her to say something about the two of us leaving together, I think.

But she didn't say anything like he wanted and she just smiled. "Did you want me to pick you up at the hotel and drop you off at the airport tomorrow?"

"Yeah," he said and there was a pause as they looked at each other. "The flight to New York's at 10:27."

"I'll pick you up a little before ten."

There was another pause that was loud even with all that music blaring around us and I wanted to say something that would let her know I was going to bed with him, but she was just sipping her drink and he said, "Fine," sort of quiet and then he looked up as if he was resolved about something and said, "All right, Saranell Birdsong, lead on."

I felt that quiver in the middle of my chest again and he took my hand. I wished it was lighter so everyone could see us leaving together and the word would be out that I was the one who took off with the famous author.

I kind of fumbled around at the top of the stairs so Jim at least once would notice, but we were outside too fast and going down the stairs to the street before I was sure too many people had seen we were going.

"I'm staying at the Royal Orleans just up the street from here," he said.

I took a deep breath and had to hurry along beside him. I'd have to remember every detail to tell Carla, and good grief, if he didn't cheer up with the joint I had in my back pocket and my bod, well, for heaven's sake, what more could an older guy want.

A VISIT FROM THE CONSUL

THE SERENADERS WERE too loud at the end of the marbled room, and most of the guests were bunched up where I was, too near the tables of lobster thermidor and boiled shrimp, too near the bar. I usually liked the cafetero tunes, the jerky love songs the serenaders rattled out on their bandolas and guitars, but somehow there in the opulent room with its metal-legged tables, its glass, its gigantic orange and green abstract, the guitar notes were false, the Spanish words out of place. The serenaders seemed quaint native types doing their tricks, singing their simple songs for the hired amusement of the gringos, and it irked, saddened me. That wasn't the way it should have been done, there, atop an isolated cliff mansion with the city spread out below like a fallen patch of starry sky, surrounded on all sides by glass that looked down on the twisting river, slightly up to the hill of the three crosses, glowing faint, neon blue against the night sky.

I accepted another glass of scotch and soda and ice and went out on the balcony. It was as crowded, the music was as loud, the air as hot, and I as uncomfortable as inside. That kind of evening always made me edgy, and some hearty American business man ready for his Colombian adventure always ended up around midnight telling me how his wife really didn't like living out of the States and didn't understand how important it was for him to be in Colombia.

I took a sip of the scotch and found a perverse satisfaction in my dislike of it. Vat 69. But I preferred whiskey sours, and even the American consul in his great, glass house couldn't get a ready supply of bourbon.

I stood looking at the three crosses. One night when a bunch of us were drinking at the Alhambra, Gonzalo had looked up at them and had told me the legend that they had been erected to keep the devil out of Cali, but that the devil was already in Cali and then couldn't get out, so was forced to turn into a woman and stay. He'd given me a knowing look and had thrown back that crazy ruffled beard of his and had laughed with great explosions of air, all teeth and beard and flaying lock of black hair.

I should have been at the Alhambra. I stood and half listened to the words along the balcony beside me, the games being played at the consul's party, and took another swallow of the scotch.

"A lovely view from here, isn't it?"

The words were spoken to me. I looked around. The host himself.

"At night with those lights down there, it is probably one of the most beautiful spots on earth." He said it musingly as if we two were alone on his balcony.

I'd heard he was good at choosing just the right nuance for any situation. And even though I was aware of the technique and the practice that went into it, I still found myself warming to it.

"You'd never know from here that that hill there was Ciloe slum or that the Plaza Caycedo was full of sleeping beggars wrapped in newspapers, would you?" He turned toward me and smiled, his round face alive to the irony.

He was good at it. It was the kind of thing I might have thought myself.

"You're the young sociologist spending most of your time in some little village out of Cali, aren't you?"

Every American in the colony was probably at his party. He must have been reading files on us all afternoon. "San Pedro. About a four-hour drive from here."

He nodded. "Other side of Buga." He took a reflective sip of his drink through his nod and then asked me some questions about what I was doing there and what the people were like, listening to me seriously as if he had some interest in and some knowledge of what I was working on.

I explained how hard it'd been at first, with all that traditional machismo, to get them to listen to anything a woman might say, but that I was making headway.

He kept nodding, and when I paused he said, "I've been meaning to visit little places like that. Sort of a good will tour on a small scale, you know. Anything we can do for American good will in our small way," he smiled, "and especially if there is already an American contact in the village." He looked at me. "What do you think? Would such a tour be worthwhile?"

"They'd love it." I expanded more than usual with the scotch, but he also made me feel comfortable, as though we had known each other for months. "Nothing the U.S. could do would make San Pedro feel more important. Their having the American consul out for a visit would be like Grass Creek, Wyoming, having the Queen of England stop by for tea."

He smiled appreciatively. "I'll be in Buga a week from Thursday at the agricultural festival. Maybe that would be a good time to see your villagers."

The way he said "your" and the scotch and the dotted lights in the velvet black city below gave me a start of pride and possession.

"Great." I tabulated fast. "That would give them time to whomp up a fresh batch of chicha for you."

"Let's say about four in the afternoon then," he said as a woman came up to him, and with a quick minimal glance at me, started speaking about the fireworks, forcing him to turn to one of the opposite hills. Some blond woman with buck teeth and a silver dress brought in obviously from the States since Colombia hadn't seen a cloth of gold or silver since Belalcazar rode through in 1536 in all his Renaissance splendor.

I moved away along the balcony, feeling more out of place than before all of a sudden, avoiding little chattering groups, looking down at the city.

A visit from the United States consul would be just about the biggest thing that ever happened in San Pedro where even Christmas came and went almost unnoticed. What a shot in the arm for those poor dirt farmers with their poor drab lives.

I finished my drink and fled, thanking the consul's wife in her black dress and pearls for a nice evening and giving my host a wave across the room which he answered with a nod of understanding and a smile.

The next morning I could hardly wait to get back on the bus to Buga and San Pedro, to get back and break the news to the thin little mayor of the village that the American consul was coming to San Pedro in less than two weeks.

I got on the bus early enough to get a window seat, packed in beside a bundled mother with a baby no less wrapped in mantles and dun-colored blankets. She carefully held a bunch of pink plastic flowers.

When I first came to Colombia I'd deplored the preference of the natives for cheap plastic junk over the artifacts they ignored, but the longer I stayed in San Pedro among the tan houses, the yellowing dust in the streets, the gold pongo trees, the browning fields of corn, the clothing that somehow turned brown with sun, dirt, and careless scorching irons, no matter what color the original cloth had been, the more I understood that an artifact was merely another earth-colored fragment of their brown lives with much less significance or joy than one branch of pink plastic roses.

The bus swayed hypnotically as it hurtled through the valley, taking black-topped, gravel, dirt roads at the same post-whizzing speed, and I could doze beside the woman and child without fear of falling into the aisle on the dusty curves. The driver dug at his ear with his index finger, oblivious to the pace and the dust clouds he'd raised on the road behind.

At about noon the mother offered me a gray gelatina from the half dozen she had in a newspaper parcel, and I took it with a simulated grateful "gracias" trying to pick the coarse hairs off the gray marshmallowy slab without seeming to. I smiled at her as my teeth sank into the dusty surface and the gummy center. I pulled it away from my mouth, the artgum-eraser-stale-marshmallow consistency stretching in awkward strings from my teeth. I nodded, thanked her again as I choked it down, trying to ignore the bristles that I knew were embedded in the center, and refused a second saying I was full already.

An hour later we reached Buga, waited around in the grimy bus station, and then climbed back on the bus that lurched off for San Pedro.

I was the only passenger for San Pedro, and the bus paused only long enough for me to get down with my canvas bag before it sped away in its great cloud of dust, the peso passengers clutching the flimsy back rails below bunches of bananas, braces of chickens strapped to the rusting top.

When I arrived at the tiny palacio where all town business was negotiated, the village men were squatting on the rough board floor, talking in low tones, waiting for the afternoon rains.

Manuel Ruiz, who had a chair, got up and offered me the seat next to Señor Escobar. If I had been a village woman, they would have ignored my presence until I went away again, but I was a gringa, and after all those months, they allowed me a place in the little room that was a male preserve.

Señor Escobar nodded to me, I sat down, and we went through the ceremonial preliminaries of remarks on the heat, the rains that would fall for a few minutes and soak into the earth without altering the state of the scorching corn, and the two women in the village who were to have babies soon, before I could speak of my two days in Cali and the singular news that the Consul americano intended to visit San Pedro.

A charge of electrified interest zigzagged around the dusky airless room, but Señor Escobar's dark face didn't change. "El Consul de los Estados Unidos shall be most welcome in our pueblo," he said in his precise Spanish, and we talked of other things.

But the next morning I saw that the activity had started. The priest, shepherd of the tiny church on the plaza whose bare wooden hall was used for the Saturday night movies, Sunday meetings, and important fiestas that might happen perhaps every three years in San Pedro, stopped by to verify the rumor, nodded importantly when I assured him that the American consul was indeed coming to the village a week from Thursday, and scurried away with black robes flapping. Baskets of corn appeared on the plaza, then disappeared inside the blank, closed doors facing the square, and I knew chicha was being prepared. The mound of pebbles, six months beside the plaza, somehow got shoveled onto the street during the week, and one morning I noticed the broken bench beneath the thick tamarind tree at the center of the plaza had been propped up on its crumbled legs and buttressed with stones for a precarious stability.

By the weekend, I could detect baking odors wafting into the breezeless plaza from the brown houses, and the Saturday night movies were called off so that the village band would not lose a night of practice in the church hall. Rodrigues Mendoza had approached me with indirect questions about the consul's food preferences, and knowing that roast pig was the most important part of any Colombian fiesta, I said emphatically that the consul was very fond of cerdo. He went away pleased with his subtle diplomacy and by Tuesday a young, whole pig had been gutted and hung inside the church hallway.

Wednesday night at the little palacio, a sense of anticipation as obvious as tinsel hung over the stained wooden floor, but the conversation remained on the heat, the approaching rainy season that would make little difference to the aridity of San Pedro, placed as it was too far from either chain of the Cordilleras for enough rain, and the oldest Blanco boy, who had found an incised pre-Colombian bowl in a ditch that afternoon.

The next morning I put on a freshly ironed skirt and blouse and caught the bus to Buga. The villagers stood in the plaza to watch me off. They said nothing and their dark thin faces shaded by woven Palmira hats expressed nothing, they just watched me climb on the bus.

I found the Agricultural Institute in Buga about noon. I knew I'd have to wait around since it was a Colombian function, but it was another two hours before I saw the group of officials, conversing with a great show of hands, coming with the American consul.

They started to pass into the office.

"Señor Adams," I said over their voices and he glanced at me.

"Hello," he said heartily and put out his hand for me to shake. "How are you?" And I knew he didn't recognize me.

I told him my name, but I could see that didn't mean anything to him either. "I . . . you . . . I'm from San Pedro," I began. Perhaps I'd mixed up the days. "You're coming to San Pedro this afternoon."

He looked at me and I thought I saw some recognition dawning on his plump face.

"The other night at your party we talked about . . . ."

"Ah, yes." He began nodding his head.

The officials of the Agricultural Institute were looking at me impatiently and I was conscious of my rumpled blouse, the dusty ride from the village. One of them opened the door to the office and put his hand on the consul's elbow.

"You said today at four you would . . . ," I began desperately.

"Ah, yes," he repeated. "I'm afraid I won't be able to make it this afternoon." He smiled that friendly smile, glancing at his wrist watch. "I have a dinner appointment this evening in Cali, and it's a three hour drive back, you know."

"But you said . . . ."

He went on as if I hadn't spoken. "But next time you're in Cali, give me a ring. I'd like to hear what you're doing out here." He gave me that nod of understanding, turned back to the officials, and smiling benignly, passed with them into the office.

I stood there in the corridor with the odor of Colombian

paste wax rising from the marble floor and then I went back outside, back to the dingy little bus station.

It was already two hours past the time I had told them we would be there when I got off the bus in the plaza.

Little Joselito Torres, obviously a lookout, didn't wait but ran toward the church hall. He disappeared inside as I started across the hot dry plaza. I noticed the hard packed earth that made up the sidewalks, the dusty leaves of the tamarind trees, the homemade American flag, uneven stars awry, draped across the church facade. And as I stepped into the rutted street of layered stones, the little band inside the church hall began their rendition of *The Star Spangled Banner,* learned in honor of the American consul from Cali.

OCTOBER AFTERNOON
CONFERENCE

SHE GAVE A perfunctory glance at the little workbook, chartreuse with vivid blue numbers under some publisher's delusion that the now children would be more attracted by bright colors, slanting, upside-down, flattened, elongated numbers than by the orderly ones of the previous generations. Man's rage for chaos in shocking chartreuse and blue on the cover, but the problems inside were the same. Neat sturdy rows of numbers, the omnipresent total line, the space for the answer in child scrawl.

"You can see he is at a level I usually expect my second graders to reach about January." The teacher's rounded globular face with its small red mouth nodded complacently. "So you know he is doing just fine."

They smiled and nodded at each other across the empty desks. She thought again how all those elementary school teachers introduced at the first PTA meeting of the year always looked like elementary school teachers with uneven hems and mouths too small for their plumped and motherly faces.

She slid her bag a little closer, trying not to show her impatience with the classroom manner. There were so many things she had to arrange that afternoon, and she'd known before hand that the little school conference would be a waste of time. There wasn't a thing the teacher could say about him she didn't already know, not a thing that the class reports hadn't already said—that he was polite and conscientious, careful, eager, had a good imagination with a tendency to extravagant "What if . . . ."

"I always have them do a little assignment centered around the holiday." The teacher's voice beamed, head bobbing, nodding. "Here's a little story I had them write just this morning. I told them it had to be about a Happy Halloween Ghost."

She held the tablet, ready to flip the page, scanned it quickly.

THE HAPPY GHOST CAME TO SEE ME ON HIS MAGIC CARPIT. HE ASKD ME IF I WANTED TO RIDE, WE WENT UP AND I LOOKED DOWN AND I THOUT I WAS JACK. THEN WE CAME BACK DOWN AND HE FLU OFF.

It jolted her and she felt her face stiffen. She kept looking down at the page and read it again.

" . . . get to draw an illustration on the back." The soothing teacher tones spread out like soapsuds around the little tablet as she turned the page.

She looked at the picture, the childlike figure in shirt and jeans, the smiling ghost floating beside him on a square that was obviously the carpet. Crosses like telephone poles lined the bottom of the page.

THOUT I WAS JACK.

Thought he was Jack.

The phrase sounded in her head louder than the flowing comforting elementary schoolroom voice.

Perhaps in the freedom of composition, in the telling of a story, what he really felt was emerging, what his deepest consciousness was saying had come out.

She sat trying to make the same correct responses, motions, smile the same as ten minutes earlier.

At last she murmured something about the nice job the school was doing and got up from the too small desk and escaped, her heels clicking in the polished school hallway, clicking clear and empty and hollow.

She went out into the gray afternoon, the sky in clotted clouds like aged pillow stuffing.

She couldn't understand why she hadn't seen it, why she hadn't noticed, detected some sign. The adoption papers would be through in less than a month.

She got to the station wagon, hearing, but closing out the child voices at recess.

What if she'd seen only what she wanted to see, heard only what she wanted to hear. He hadn't mentioned Jack since last Christmas when the presents came in slick-papered department store wrappings. He never asked about him, he always referred to Nathan as his father. The papers had gone through smoothly without flaw, signed without balk, easily, properly, and the adoption would be finished by the end of the month. But what if in the depth of his second grade mind he did have reservations about relinquishing his natural father, about taking another with another name, reservations printed out almost unconsciously in the fat red school tablet.

She drove in the driveway and carried her purse in the house without putting away the car.

She smelled the new wax on the kitchen floor almost with irritation. What if the interior, something deep inside, was frayed and warping while she'd been keeping a neat and spotless house. What if what she was doing was all wrong and would do irreparable harm to him.

The rest of the afternoon she stood at the window, tried to rehearse the details of his relationship with Nathan, his lack of acquaintance with Jack whom he hadn't seen in three years. The sky stayed still and gray, the clouds hunched, folded against the coming rain.

She couldn't seem to focus, to pinpoint anything she hadn't seen before.

Perhaps the telephone poles were those on the way to San Francisco where his natural father lived.

Or perhaps he'd written "Jack" and meant "Jim," a friend of Nathan's who'd taken them up in a private plane last Thanksgiving. Flying on a carpet, feeling like a private plane, confusing the names reducing their importance.

She made a cup of instant coffee, but then stood restlessly stirring it, gazing at the steam and bubbles without tasting it.

Perhaps they should call off the adoption and wait a few years until they were sure he didn't have any deep regrets.

She was still standing by the smooth kitchen cabinets, still unresolved when he slammed through the door from his den meeting, his cub scout cap tilted sweaty over his forehead.

"What can I have for a snack?"

She suggested, rather brightly, an apple or a twinkie as he dug in his pocket for a scarf-slide fashioned from plaster in the shape of a bat.

"I went to school today," she said toward him.

He was admiring the bat. "What?"

She repeated it and he nodded.

"I saw the little Halloween assignment you did this morning."

"The what?"

"The Halloween story you wrote."

"Oh." He piled his lunch box, cap, slide, scarf in the wicker rocker.

"I thought it was nice." She wondered if he was still listening.

"Did you see the picture?"

"I liked all the telephone poles."

"The squashy boxes were houses."

She nodded. "And who was that you felt like? A Jim . . . or . . .?" She dragged it out, hesitating, letting him interrupt.

"Jack. Like Jack in the Beanstalk. You know, way up high."

"Oh, of course," she said.

MRS. JESSIE MARTHA JONES

"MISS JESSIE MARTHA, can you hear me?"

Of course she could hear them. Banging the bedpan, the ice pitcher, the lot of them like a herd of rooting pigs and then shouting at her, his mouth almost down on the pillow beside her ear.

But she kept her body still as she could and her eyes closed against all their noise, hoping they'd go away and let her think.

"I can't understand it. There's nothing I can find wrong with her."

Of course those young fool doctors couldn't understand anything.

"She hasn't touched a single tray in the last four days, doctor."

She kept her eyes shut, not too tight so they'd know she was able to do it and was keeping them out on purpose, but just loose shut, black shut against them.

"Try to get her to eat something. Does there seem to be anything special she likes?"

A withering sigh seeped into her darkness.

"You know how these older colored people are, doctor, what with . . . ."

She stopped listening. She knew how to do that. Poor white trash having to work for a living in a nursing home. She'd never had to work. Her Daddy had seen to that. Before she was married and then when Earl John ran off with that piece of baggage, . . . no, "ran off " wasn't the word, it wasn't like it was something he'd wanted to do. Her Daddy hadn't raised her to be working out, and Earl John himself always said she should wear white silk dresses and sit on the mohair sofa like he'd seen her the first time when he came to call on her Daddy. She'd go to commencement every year in a new white silk dress with a floppy garden hat on her pressed hair that was pulled back straight and neat, not the way her Ivoria was wearing it now-a-days in that Afro thing that made her look so trashy. She'd arrive on the dot of nine o'clock at the chapel and as soon as she was in her seat, they'd start the commencement march. She could always hear the whispers running through the chapel hall as she came up the side aisle, "Here comes Jessie Martha," "There's Jessie Martha now," and then they'd start the march. Every year in the spring, even after Earl John had gone, right on the button at 9:00 sharp in a new white silk dress and petticoat and a new big white garden hat each year that . . . .

"Well, try to get her to eat something, or at least drink some water or juice. I hate to go intravenous on these old people."

Lord Jesus, they were still there in the room hovering around her bed like August flies. Why didn't they go bother somebody else.

She felt a clumsy heavy pat on her shoulder that almost crackled her skin.

"Miss Jessie Martha, you eat something today, you hear."

She didn't open her eyes as she heard him go out. She listened to hear if that nurse went too, but sometimes she missed those squishy shoes and she didn't want to open her eyes yet. Well, let her stay if that's what she wants to do with her time.

It got hard to get white silk, real silk, after the war started. That was about the time Earl John left. Yes, it was during the war when Earl John was gone that she'd had to start buying synthetic materials to have her dresses made from. Her Daddy said they were just as pretty as the real silk ones and that she was as pretty as a picture in them too, but somehow it wasn't the same, not having the real silk dresses to wear to the graduation ceremony every June, like not being really married any more after a while even though Earl John never got a divorce but just went off to live with that woman and let her have all those children in every shade of yellow brown.

Earl John had such dark skin it was a wonder more of those children didn't come out dark. Would have served them right. It was good Ivoria took after her and not Earl John, and when he'd insisted on the name he'd picked out it was like he knew she was going to be the only light-skinned child he'd have.

It was as if the war that took away the white silk took away her marriage. Earl John left and went off to the Navy, and just never came back.

Oh, he came back from the war all right, she nodded behind her closed eyes, but when he came back to her Daddy's great white house just off campus where she'd been living while he was away, he said, "I don't want to be no

Negro college president like your Daddy, making up to the Man to be my own man." She never could break him of those double negatives no matter how hard she tried. "Come with me," he'd said. "We can make it away from your Daddy," but she didn't understand what he was talking about, and her Daddy said the best thing to do with a man was just ignore whatever was bothering him, just let him have a little rein, don't hold on too tight, just stay put in the white house till he'd sowed a few oats. And then when he went to live with that woman, it was only that . . . .

"See what you can do. She hasn't even taken a sip of water in three days now. It's like she's trying to starve herself to death."

"What for?"

"How should I know?"

Of course she wouldn't know. Not anything, not any of them.

But it wasn't like she was trying to starve herself, it was just that . . . .

"Miss Jessie Martha, I have some nice soup here."

All of them calling her "Miss." Not a one of them knew anything about anything.

"Miss Jessie Martha?"

It was one of those nurses aides with those hesitant voices you didn't need to do anything for because they were so uneasy about their own shadows that they'd never force you to do something if you didn't want to, and they'd never call the doctors to have them tell you to do whatever it was they wanted. You could always ignore the nurses aides like that one. It was probably the terrible chicken soup anyway that tasted of the metal urn they cooked it in down at the kitchen.

All of a sudden she felt herself smiling inside thinking of Earl John's Uncle Enid cooking in the big white kitchen of Central Hospital where none of the colored were admitted, making a point to spit in the gravy, a great mouthful of saliva right in the cream gravy for all those sick white folks upstairs. He was so like Earl John, the same . . . .

"Miss Jessie Martha?"

They couldn't understand. When Ivoria got back from Earl John's funeral, she said he had on his bedside table that little picture of her holding Ivoria her Daddy had taken while he was away in the Navy. She'd sent it to him in the Pacific, and she remembered wondering if he'd ever get it. But he did. Then when he'd gone off with that woman, she'd waited, and when Ivoria told her about the picture, right beside his bed, she knew she'd been right in waiting, no matter what her Daddy said. It was the one time she'd stood up against her Daddy when he wanted her to get a divorce and look around the college for someone else. Twenty-seven years and four months Earl John'd been gone from her Daddy's house, but he didn't get a divorce and she'd known all that time he'd be back.

"Well, let it go then. There are too many patients on this hall that do need . . . ."

She heard them out in the hall, was sure they were gone, and opened her eyes. But it was too bright and she didn't want to see her withered hands lying dark on the white flocked coverlet. Her lids were heavy and she let them drop back shut. The darkness was better to wait for Earl John. His skin was so dark against the white suits and two-tone white and black shoes he always fancied. He was such a handsome man, it was no wonder so many women were after him and he had to look at them once in a while. Her Daddy'd never understood that. But she knew all that time he'd be back. She'd put on a white silk dress, real silk, and sit on the mohair sofa like that very first time he came through the door of her Daddy's . . . .

AN EVENING'S SEDUCTION

"ARE YOU READY to go to bed?"

"What?" He paused with his coffee cup midway to his mouth.

"Are you ready to go to bed now?"

He sat there with the cup stopped in the air between his lips and the table, extended, the steam rising in a faint lazy swirl. Then he set it carefully back in the saucer and looked at her over the candles. "Let's try that one more time. What did you say?"

"I asked if you were ready to go to bed, to make love to me now."

"I thought that's what you said."

"We've finished the meal, and I thought perhaps you'd like to go to bed first and then later we could have an after-dinner liqueur by the fire."

"I guess I hadn't thought about it just yet." He started to

pick up his cup again but then he reached in his pocket and brought out a cigarette instead. He didn't look at her as he leaned toward one of the candles to light it.

"I didn't know you smoked. I don't have any ashtrays out."

He waved his hand. "I'm quitting. It's just that sometimes I need . . . . After dinner sometimes . . . ." He put it out on the side of his plate and the ashes slid into the congealing remains of the steak juices.

"Didn't you think about laying me when I invited you over to dinner tonight? Isn't that what most guys think when they go over to a single girl's apartment?"

"I guess so in a way. It's just that . . . ."

"I thought it would save a lot of time, a lot of the game playing our society is so riddled with if we just brought it out in the open. I think this whole sex role thing could be taken care of so easily if men and women would just be honest with each other." She flipped her hair back as she talked and it trailed over her shoulder.

He nodded slightly.

"Well?"

"Hugnh?"

"Are you ready to go to bed?"

"I guess so." He got up heavily, dropping his napkin off his lap. He saw it on the carpet, started to pick it up and then didn't and pushed his chair back further from the table. His sleeve caught briefly in the spoked back of the dining chair.

She leaned over to blow out the two candles on the table. Her long hair fell forward again.

"Up these stairs." She led the way.

"Oh, yeah. I forgot these were town houses." His voice wavered near the casual.

A hanging swag lamp over the bed sent out enough light to read by.

She went over to the mirror, took off the coils of plastic necklaces she had around her neck and dumped them on the dresser.

"Uh, do we need that much light on?" He indicated the bright purple globe of the lamp. He was unbuttoning his jacket.

"Oh." She glanced up, turned on one of the little milk glass night lights on the dresser, and clicked off the overhead light without moving from in front of the mirror. "That better?"

"Fine." He put his jacket and tie over the back of a chair and started working at the tiny buttons of his shirt. He watched her unzip her long hostess skirt and step out of it. She didn't have on stockings or panty hose.

She slid her blouse off over her head, dropped it on the skirt still in a heap on the shag rug, then her bra and panties, without moving from the dresser. She stood there nude, turned down the bed, and got in on one side.

He was only at his belt and she lay there and watched him while he took off his pants and shorts and put them on the chair. He tried to take off his shoes standing up, but he kept teetering from side to side and had to sit down on his pants.

When he got to the bed, she pulled back the covers for him, exposing a haze of bare pink flesh as he climbed in beside her.

"That's nice. I like men with lots of hair." She reached over and touched her fingers to his neck and drew them down to his stomach. Her red nail polish caught the glow of the little lamp.

He lay there and she propped on an elbow beside him, her breasts barely touching his chest.

Then he turned to face her.

"Hi."

"Hi."

He put an arm around her and ran his hand along her side.
She lay back and he kissed her, her mouth opening under
his. He rolled over on top of her and kept kissing her. She
had both arms around his neck drawing him down, holding
him.

He kissed her chin, her neck, beside her ear, stroking her
arm, her breast. He raised up slightly and ran his hand
through her hair.

"What's the matter?"

"Nothing."

He kissed her again, his tongue meeting hers and their lips
clung together, the juices of their mouths mingling.

Then she pulled her head back into the pillow, turning it
aside from his face.

"What's wrong?"

He rolled off and lay beside her. "I guess I just wasn't
quite ready."

"What do you mean?'

"Well, you know, a guy . . . ." He turned over on his
back again and looked up at the ceiling. Each link in the
brass chain of the hanging lamp reflected a little milk glass
light. " . . . a guy sort of has to take the initiative in a thing
like this."

"But that's silly." She sat up, the sheet and quilted satin
spread dropping to her waist. "For decades women have
been inviting men to dinner and they'd sit around over
drinks and grope and neck and finally he'd work off her
clothes and screw her on the living room floor or some-
place."

He put his arm across his forehead, shading his eyes.

"I thought we'd gotten away from those kind of nonsen-
sical roles where the man has to be the conquering hero and
the little woman the complaisant conquest. That's what this
liberation is all about, isn't it?"

"Yeah, I guess so."

"But then . . . ." She waited for him to look at her, to say something.

"It's just that you . . . can't really do it this way." He kept his arm over his face and swept his other hand out to include the room.

She sat there and looked down at him.

"But then all this Women's Lib isn't worth anything, is it?"

He didn't look out from under his arm. "I guess not," he said.

THE WITCH OF
PEACH TREE STREET

I WASN'T BILLED that way, of course. Actually I wasn't
billed at all. I just sat on one of those high bar stools in the
Jester Club until someone called me over to read their cards,
scan their palm or sometimes just read their jewelry, tell
where the piece came from or what happened to whoever
gave it or owned it last, that sort of thing. Al Gagliardo liked
having me there, said it gave the place a certain class to have
a psychic around. And I'm good at it. When I'm really with
the vibrations, really in tune, I can hit about 95% accuracy
in a reading.

There in the Jester's Club it's mostly men who want me
to read for them, and I'll admit I'd rather work with men
who can be real believers when it comes right down to the
wire, but that one night it was the two women who got to
me, those two women about half an hour apart, not with
each other but linked in a way I could feel even before I cut
the cards for the second one.

The first one came in by herself about eight, early before anyone was there much, and she was noticeable for the J.C. because she was so unnoticeable if you know what I mean. She had on a beige suit, the kind of thing with a dyed-to-match mink collar that ladies wear, and I could tell her husband didn't like her to wear anything but beiges, tans, browns, an occasional dark green, because nothing else is really lady-like.

She came straight over to where I was perched at the end of the bar, not drinking because that can blur the signals, but just sitting and watching Johnny Mac cut up oranges to make slices for whiskey sours. She came straight over and said, "I need to have my fortune told." Not "I want" or "I'd like," but "I *need*."

I said okay and we went over to one of the little tables with a candle already lit in the hurricane lamp, and she ordered a gin and tonic. They don't have to order anything to have me read, and Al keeps saying I'm not there to jack up the sales like serving peanuts with your beer, but they almost always do order something. It makes everybody more comfortable, more sociable, makes having your fortune told more like a party game.

She took off the jacket to the suit with the mink collar and I saw she had on an opera length string of real pearls.

"You live uptown," I said. That wasn't a guess, even though the probability was good that her type would live uptown, but I could see it like a superimposed picture over her, the whitewash of the old brick on her antebellum house, even as I looked at her.

She just watched me over the rim of her glass, her eyes picking up the points of the candle, doubling it in her pupils. I didn't mind. A lot of them do that, waiting to see what you're going to show them before they'll commit themselves with even a nod.

"I'll cut the cards and you lay them in five piles. The

person who is to be read should handle the pack and let his individual vibrations send the cards into the proper stacks that will reveal the past, present, and future. There is nothing haphazard, only figures bound magically to the diviner and the inquirer." I always give them that, but it doesn't really make that much difference; you don't even need cards to tell the future for most people.

She put her drink down and did what I told her still without saying anything or betraying the slightest agreement or disagreement. She was careful, neat, and I could see her living room full of polished, dusted antiques with needlepoint cushions. Her diamond engagement ring was small, neat the same way, and I know her husband had given it to her before he'd made it big.

I laid out the cards face up.

She was so orderly that the cards came out like a stacked deck. And of course I could see at once why she needed them read. I put them all out and sat looking down at them in the candlelight. Her husband was an architect or a lawyer, I couldn't tell which.

"Well?"

I glanced up at her. "You want to know if your husband will find out."

This time she nodded.

"You knew that before you came in, but you wanted me to tell you when."

Another nod.

"He'll find out this month." I covered the three outside cards with those from the inner row. "Two years has been a pretty long affair for him not to have found out before now." I touched the new top card with my fingernail and it clicked. "This is the Tower, the destruction card."

She was watching me eagerly, and I knew she'd been wanting what was going to happen to happen for a long time.

"It'll probably be a Wednesday afternoon."

"Will he do anything violent?"

"No." I stacked the cards and shuffled them. "He's not the violent type."

She mumbled something that sounded like "I know" and sipped her drink.

"It hasn't happened yet, and you can always alter the future, you know. It doesn't have to happen that way."

She looked at me and I knew she wanted it to happen that way, wanted him to walk in on the two of them in bed.

"He isn't seeing her any more according to these," I said toward the deck. "It's been over for quite a while between them I'd guess."

She just looked at me.

I shrugged slightly. You can't change what's already happened for any of them, and you can't give them any advice.

She was putting back on the jacket, the dyed mink up around her chin like an animal. "How much is this?"

"Whatever you feel the reading is worth."

She buttoned the buttons very neatly, slowly and correctly, opened the expensive alligator purse and then a billfold and laid a bill on the table. "Thank you." She stood up.

"Thank you," I echoed without looking at the bill. It doesn't matter then after you've made the stand. You have to take whatever they put down.

She went out without glancing around, straight out without a waver or a pause.

I picked up the bill. It was a twenty.

I wondered what it'd have been if I'd told her the rest of it I saw in the cards, about his being black, her lover. I wondered if she'd wanted me to know about that part, wanted me to articulate it so she could savor it twice before her husband found out. I supposed he would have to be black to really get back at a Southerner like her husband was bound to be.

I was still sitting there at the same table when the second one came in.

I knew right away there was something, some tie-in with that first one, but I couldn't put my finger on it because the first one wasn't pregnant and the second one was.

She didn't show yet, but she knew about it and that wasn't what she'd come in for.

She was different from the other one in that she belonged in the Jester's Club. People that come in and really belong are pretty much of a type, business men, secretaries, career women, and this one was one of those, stylish, assured, somebody's mistress.

She came over and shook her head at Johnny Mac when he got up to see if she wanted anything to drink.

I motioned to a chair and she sat down.

I cut the deck and handed it to her and she put them in the five piles like she'd done it before.

They were about the same age, and I could see the lines deep around her eyes there in the candlelight, but they weren't friends, and it was something else pulling the two of them together in my mind.

I started turning the cards over, spreading them out.

When I turned it up I almost jerked my hand back, dropping the rest of them. But I've been in the business long enough, and I went on, putting them in stacks, face up, and I was pretty sure she didn't notice anything.

But you don't see a death card very often. And there it was staring up at me, hard and slick, catching all the candlelight from the hurricane lamp as if it were the only card on the table.

I leaned back to get the glare off the card. "You've been married only a little while." But it was one of those marriages that you almost don't believe in any more, the real thing, you know.

She smiled and unconsciously touched the underside of her wedding ring with her thumb.

The past lay there to the side and I could see she'd been somebody's mistress all right, for a long time. A dapper little man, buttoned up and wanting to be taller than he was. He'd ended it and she'd even tried suicide with pills that didn't work, but I turned the past cards over and looked back at her present.

"You waited a long time."

It was the kind of marriage you wanted to see last a long time.

"What's that card there?" she said.

She touched it and her nails were pale, buffed.

A lot of people do that, in fact more people than you'd think. They come in to have me confirm what they already suspect.

I looked at her and she knew and she knew I knew.

"Have you ever thought of an abortion?"

"Oh, no."

"He's never had any children?"

She shook her head. "His first wife died of cancer, you know."

I nodded.

"It's a boy ," I said pointing to a card.

"He'll like that."

We sat there with the death card between us on the table. She didn't really want to hear about anything else. You can't tell them about things that'll go beyond themselves, the things that'll go on without them there. They don't want to hear about the world that'll survive when they're gone.

She got up and put a bill on the table.

"No, please I . . . ."

"Don't be silly." She put it under a card and turned away.

I watched her out the door that opened onto Peach Tree and saw the neon around her silhouette, a blue red glow around her from the jester sign out front, and then I put the bill in my pocket without looking at it.

I went over to the end of the bar. "I'll have a bourbon and water."

"I'm glad it's not one of them lady drinks."

I brushed my hand at him.

A death card always shakes me up.

When Johnny Mac brought the drink, I sat there sipping it, something nagging at me.

Then it hit me.

I hadn't been that concerned with past, that pile of cards, but as I saw them again in my head, I recognized the architect-lawyer, the kind all buttoned up that marries a pale beige virgin and keeps a career woman on the side, the white maiden you marry and the dark lady you don't.

I took a long swallow of the bourbon and water.

What a waste.

I was glad he was going to get that Wednesday after all.

"I hear you're pretty good with that pack of cards." A hand tapped my shoulder.

I turned and looked at him.

A fleshy middle thirties, with a college ring on his right hand, a wedding band on his left, who wanted to be a few inches taller and who'd probably had only a couple of girls before he'd married and felt cheated and trapped. I could tell by the look in his eyes that he was figuring this was a good place to find a girl for the few days he was going to be in town.

"It's probably as good a place as any," I said.

He looked a little startled and then tried to cover it with a jaunty smirk. "I have a table over ther. What're you drinking?" He indicated my glass.

"I don't drink." I picked up the deck of cards that wouldn't tell me a damn thing about him I didn't already know and led the way to the table.

RITE OF PASSAGE

I WATCHED HER sip the sweet pink, mildly nauseous Postobon.

"Wouldn't you rather have a beer?"

She took her mouth away from the bottle and her lips were moist. She shook her head and smiled in a way that made me think of maraschino cherries. "I don't like hot beer very well."

And I knew she didn't drink beer at all. Naturally not. I almost sighed audibly and took a swallow of my warm flat beer.

Her blue-eyed gaze waited for me to pick up the frayed thread of our conversation, a gaze so clear and clean and innocent, I felt tired, old, just looking at her.

"Have you been absorbing the local color while you've been here?" I wasn't up to hearing about her project just then.

"Isn't this place just beautiful? With the river and the jungle. So really lovely." She leaned forward eagerly , with probably the same eagerness she'd have used for anything I said, the perfect student. "Do you anthropologists call it 'local color,' too?"

"A layman's term." I managed a smile. Why do blue eyes look so naive? Sapphire universals of good and fair opposed to seed black evil. I looked at her porcelain blondness, the Wedgewood blue-eyedness of her, set down beside the dark, sun-baked Colombians.

"Some of the local people were telling me about a ceremony upriver that's supposed to be fabulous. For an Indian girl's coming of age. Do you know about it?"

She was innocently proud of her inside knowledge, her personal commerce with the local people, letting me know neither subtly nor unkindly that she lived in the pueblo with them, that I was merely visiting out of Bogotá.

I nodded.

"Manuel Ortigas is going up river tomorrow morning. Would you like to go and see the ceremony?"

I assured her I would, and we made small talk about the beauties of the village and the river while she finished the sweet soda water and I had another tepid beer. As she talked I marveled that she was able to expound on the setting and the people without once using words like "exotic" or "strange." I wondered if they were taboo in the Peace Corps booklet, or if in her type of naiveté everything was equally new and nothing really ever strange. At any rate, we parted with plans for the morning, and I escaped without having heard her particular project.

The next morning I was a little more steeled for it, and her, as we climbed into the dugout. She sat next to me and something about her even in her khakis and Indian sandals reminded me of roseate caramel apples.

Manuel Ortigas started the motor with a kick and a two-handed jerk that bounced the dugout forward and coughed out about half the life of the engine, and we were off upriver.

As the meditative green shade of the jungle closed in around us, she gazed at it and turned to me with that trusting blue look. "Have you ever noticed how artificial the jungle looks? Sort of too green, over-arranged somehow?"

I looked at her with surprised interest until she added, "Hawthorne says that kind of nature is evil, and when you look at this jungle I think he might be right, don't you?"

Hawthorne, of course, probably junior year. I added something noncommital about the jungle and Hawthorne and then said, "Tell me about your project in the village."

"I'm working on community development." She turned to me eagerly. "And starting on something fairly small, you know, but important from a hygienic standpoint, I'm trying to teach the village mothers to put diapers on their babies. Particularly the toddlers. I think the cleanliness of the house and then the whole village might be approached from that one point, don't you?"

I looked thoughtful. It was as bad as I'd anticipated. The uselessness of sending these young kids out into the bush with no training, no skills. The brilliant come-on of advertisements showing Peace Corps youths building bridges in Tanganyika or revolutionizing farming methods in Taiwan, and then shipping off the youngsters fresh out of school with their blue-eyed dewiness intact, their helpless lack of knowledge untouched. I couldn't sit there in the dugout and tell her that diapers would only make more clothes, more work for the already over-worked village mothers beside their soapless rocky streams, or that half-naked Colombian toddlers were trained by the lack of diapers. I couldn't tell her that her concept of the unsanitary was not necessarily that of rural Colombia.

So I didn't say anything and she elaborated on how she was contacting a few village mothers at a time. I gave a semblance of listening and watched the banks skim by us, the twisted choking vines flicking past as if alive. She was still explaining what she planned for the village, a step at a time of course, when Manuel Ortigas beached the dugout beside a ragged collection of grass huts.

Few villagers came down to the river bank to greet us, but those who did were beaming happily and informed us that the party was ready.

We were ushered to a grassy knoll where an entire wild pig, head and teeth as well as crisped tail, was roasting over a pit fire with some smaller bony animals I identified as monkeys. The women sat at one side around a great two-handled copper cooking pot chewing corn, spitting mangled kernels coated with their strings of saliva in the pot, making new chicha that would ferment as the party continued over the next few days.

Manuel Ortigas joined the men beside the roasting, grease-dripping pig and I went over to the side with my little glass Peace-Corps-ingenue. I wondered how much she really knew about the puberty rite we'd come to see.

I was beginning to feel awkward among the busy village women and started pointing out the arrangement of the huts, their peaked-roof construction, the basic industry of the Indian river village, which was the production of manioc. As I explained the whole process of squeezing the prussic acid from the manioc root and then grinding the mass into a farina flour, she listened brightly, expectantly, her blue eyes fixed in turn on the mangy huts, the manioc basket dangling from its tree, the half-filled metates abandoned for the party. She managed to make me feel wise, old, and somehow inately foolish all at the same time, but I was able to stall until the wild pig was ready and one of the villagers brought us each a leaf of the hot, greasy meat.

She accepted with gracious Spanish phrases the Indians didn't understand and nibbled at the edges of the gamey pork. She did the same with the tasteless boiled plantains, the sweet monkey, and the saltless farina bread, as she gazed at everything with her mirror-blue eyes.

At last we were shown to a sun-dried area freshly cleared for the occasion, and I could see beyond the bamboo hut-cage where the girl had been kept before the party. I'd known some of those rites to keep the girl away from the village for weeks while the family painted the masks, carved shell necklaces, wove baskets, and cooked the feast. No coming-out party in the States was ever more elaborately planned, and sometimes I was even convinced the results were the same.

We were seated with the rest of the guests in a loose circle around the clearing, and the chicha began to flow.

Served in hollowed half-gourd bowls, the raw chicha fermentation smelled of cellar vegetables as I tasted it. It was sour and cloudy, admittedly bad, but enough of it was potent, and that was what counted.

As the bowls went around again, the music started. Calloused fingers thumped the beat on stretched leather drum heads, chipped on raspas in time to the musicians' high-pitched, tuneless moan, a repeated strain of "E-e-e-e-e-e, d-e-e-e-e-e-e-e, e-e-e-e-e-e-e, d-e-e-e-e-e-e-e," as more chicha was poured and drunk.

The young college girl lifted the gourd bowl to her lips and smiled at the villagers, but I didn't ever see her swallow.

The guest of honor, the maiden in her puberty, was a plump teen with shining black eyes and filed teeth that pointed forward as she grinned around the circle. Centered on a painted mat, she sat glowing in her new pink cotton shift, brought all the way from Letitia, and giggled over her chicha.

The late afternoon sunlight slanted across the river gallery forest and the villagers swayed to the tuneless music. The girl began to giggle more loosely, the leather beat quickened, and the men began putting on their masks.

Bark cloth and balsa, carved into a toothy, heavily-browed face, accented with tar and coconut fur, the masks slipped over the men's heads, the sleeve of bark cloth covering their necks and shoulders, and the clearing became ringed with the fierce blank stare of ritual.

Then at some signal I'd never been able to catch, four men bounded up from their places around the circle, dashed in a drunken wavering run toward the girl on her center mat, grabbed a handful of her hair, and ran back to their places with the triumphant swatch. Then the next group of men in their leering masks made the same dash, pulled out their handful of hair from the head of the giggling girl, and ran back to the circle, all in time to the beat and the high-pitched plaint of the singers.

I glanced at the Peace Corps girl. Her fingers were locked, her face pale, and her blue eyes wide. I wagered then she hadn't known anything about the ceremony.

But I had to give her credit. I could see the surprise and near horror all over her face, but she had enough guts to sit there watching, trying to be polite. She probably needn't have bothered, the villagers being too drunk or engrossed in the ceremony to notice what she did, but she sat there stiff and still.

Finally the last group of maskers had a run at the girl and she'd been literally snatched bald-headed as she sat smiling happily, weaving on her mat, the center of attention, the guest of honor who would be a woman when her hair grew back.

I wanted to tell my white-faced American companion

that the girl had been so anesthetized by the chicha she probably didn't feel a thing, but I decided my saying something might be worse than nothing at all, and I merely got her out of the circle and dragged Manuel down to the beached dugout.

As we headed back downriver, she sat in the wooden canoe with her face blanched and her blue eyes not quite so sparkling in the fading light. We rode in silence with only the sound of the outboard motor breaking the dark jungle stillness.

The sudden tropical night had dropped over us by the time we beached. I told her good-bye and good luck, and she smiled a little wanly as she walked away toward the adobe house where she lived with a local family. I had to give her credit though, she was game.

I went into the little hotel cantina and ordered a warm beer.

Manuel Ortigas came in and joined me at the little hacked, worn table with his own beer and scummy glass.

"You and the little Peace Body enjoy the party this afternoon, verdad?" he asked, translating literally from the English into Spanish.

I nodded. "Muy interesante."

He smiled happily to have pleased me and then he leaned forward confidentially. "La Peace Body is a nice señorita," he said. "We here in the village try to help her all we can."

I looked at him in his khaki shirt and pants that were his only pair, his Indian-woven slippers with soles cut from old Goodyear tires, and I knew then what the kids were contributing. Not highways, not improved livestock techniques, but something more important. No one is quite so helped as when he's helping, and no technical knowledge could possibly compete with her ice-cream innocence.

I sipped my tepid beer and wondered how the U.S. government had tumbled to that one.

ANDREW'S MISTRESS

THE HOUSE WAS veiled with roses like the illustration in a child's primer. Bursting, bulging, crowding roses, yellows, pinks, reds, talismans, tangling in hedges, pulling at trellises, dragging against branches too slim for them, swaying almost high as the once white columns. Every morning you drove down Washington, past the mouldering cemetery with its ivy draped oven graves, into the Garden District, you could see her out working, clipping, tying, watering in a city that didn't need water, making the roses bloom, bud, bloom again, long past their season. You could see her, the great drooping prewar hat shading her face, the lemon-colored dog beside her, as familiar a morning sight as the black waiter in his white coat across the street washing down the sidewalk in front of Commander's Palace. She always glanced up and waved, and then you could see the make-up layered white, the red spot on each cheek, the scarlet gash of the mouth.

In the afternoons she disappeared inside. Into the house that differed only by the wall of roses from the other two of its triplets known as Freret's Folly, the three identical columned mansions that had sat empty from the Civil War until Andrew bought the center one for her in the twenties.

I went up the jagged broken walk between the gauntlet of roses. Buds, opening blossoms, full-blown browning petals, empty stems, iron thorns, all dropping tiny globes of water. Hanging strands of miniature reds touched my shoulder, my ankles, left tiny wet trails on my bare arm, my stockinged bone.

But when I got through all the dampness to the house, it was dry.

Humped on rotting cyprus pilings and leaf mulch that was the ground, the house itself was crumbling, flaking dry. Hot baked paint peeling in long strips from the columns, dried wood scars, scabs, puffed blisters of paint on the porch and door, the lentil-sized bell, hot dry metal.

I pushed it and heard the sound inside the house, far inside, well deep.

I waited, then pressed it again, listening to the hollow metal of the chimes. I more than half hoped she'd forgotten or had gone out, but I knew she hadn't. She never went out.

Then I heard footsteps. Faint and light on bare floors. It was just as well. I'd put off a visit too many times.

The footsteps came louder, closer, across the entryway.

There was a metal rasp of a chainlock, another, and finally a turning latch.

The door opened, but I couldn't see her for a moment.

"Why, Patsy, don't you look nice!" She opened the door wider.

It always gave me a start to hear that name. As if my long dead grandmother were noticing me in that same Southern voice.

I could see the red discs of rouge on her cheeks, lipstick splashed across her mouth, pink dangling hoop earrings, pink shirt-waist cotton wrinkled and too long, rosetted ballet house slippers over anklets.

"Come in Patsy. We were just fixing the tea tray." One more tug at the door and I went into the dusk of the room.

"I thought we would have tea in the morning room. The view of the garden is so pleasant this time of day. I have some of my special purple roses out now, and you can see all the new buds I have just beginning. Come along now, and we can talk while I finish up the tea things. What a lovely dress. So cool and light for this dreadful weather. Hasn't it been just awful? I know how you must . . . ."

I didn't need to say anything as I followed her through the empty rooms. Her words fell into the emptiness with the same light clicks Charlie Pepper, the lemon-colored dog, made with his nails on the wooden floors, as if her words would keep me from noticing the rooms.

We went from the vestibule to the vacant parlor, into the empty dining room.

Once the rooms had been carpeted, crowded with antebellum mahogany suites, Georgian walnut pieces, velvet love seats whose cushions clouded around you as you sat down. But now even the chandeliers were gone, and two black wires arched stiff pronged from holes in the ceilings. In the dining room one small pie crust table stood between the windows, the only piece in the room, holding a crowd of figurines balanced together in dust so thick I couldn't tell where their glass stopped and the wood began.

I hadn't realized she'd sold off so much.

We went into the kitchen where there was an ancient legged stove, refrigerator, kitchen table and stools, linoleum with worn holes meshing black into the wood beneath.

"Why don't you sit right here and tell me all about what you've been doing. Let's see, it's been how long?" She scooped up a pile of newspapers from one of the kitchen stools and put them carefully, without seeming to, over an obvious rend in the linoleum. "This won't take a minute."

I mentioned some minor happenings from previous weeks, and she smiled and nodded while she poured hot water in a chipped fluted china pot, clapped on the painted china lid.

I noticed she still had her rings. The old-fashioned gold dome with intertwined sapphires and rubies, the platinum and diamond dinner ring, the sunburst of emeralds he'd given her last, when she was still his secretary-mistress. I remembered her with them on her manicured right hand, diamond studs in her ears, matched green suits and pumps or rose or blue that picked up the flash of the stones. Flaunting them all at the same time on the same hand for us to see at family open houses and holidays, letting us know how much she meant to him, letting us know they'd have married if he could have divorced. Rings all on her right hand, even now, since his wife was still alive.

She put dainty napkins, forks, and two plates each with a slice of cake on the tray.

I was glad there were only two.

"Let me carry that, Aunt Lilla." She liked me to call her that even though she was only a cousin by marriage to my mother.

She smiled the way my grandmother might have smiled, but the white make-up grimaced, echoed her mouth in lines, circles like water rings around a leaf.

I took it into the little morning room off the kitchen and put it on the one table.

There were still tired drapes at the French doors and a sideboard stood against the wall with hundreds of dusty glass flowers, painted vases, china girls, pin cushion hearts stuck with threaded needles, tiny bottles, demitasse cups, saucers in wire holders. Probably all the bric-a-brac from the front rooms, piled, cleared from tables and buffets as they were sold.

Above it was an oval-framed photograph, brown and faded, of Andrew in a World War I uniform.

She followed my glance as she sat down in one of the two chairs. "That's Andrew the first year we met," she smiled. He's resting right now, but he'll join us later. He's so anxious to see you."

I was in no hurry. I'd never really liked Andrew. He'd always disturbed me somehow when she'd brought him around for family gatherings. Heavily aristocratic with his blue eyes numbering our furnishings, tabulating our worth almost automatically. Tall and broad, seeming even taller and broader than he was in the white seersucker suits, watching the sharp afternoon rains from the veranda. Knowing with prideful disdain all the plantations along the Mississippi crescent, owning, managing, controlling acres upon acres of sugar and cotton land, calling Lilla "Beauty" with a condescending affection as if he owned her too. Never once mentioning his wife, his sons, although we all knew about them, and we'd all felt he was using Lilla, even before his moving in with her, away from his family, the wife, the sons, even before his stroke.

She poured a cup of tea. "Oh, perfect," as she studied it. "I'm getting so forgetful, I almost always get it too strong. And you know how Andrew just can't stand something that isn't just right."

I remembered his demand for another pot of tea when his cup got too cold. Not a refill, but an entire rebrewed teapot if his cup of tea was too cold.

She passed out the little napkins, cake and forks, businesslike, brisk, the way she probably stacked the long ago cotton invoices in his offices.

"How's your mother doing?"

"They think it may be cancer."

"Oh, dear."

I let her murmur the platitudes of hopefulness and took a bite of cake.

It was powdery, tasteless, thick dust ashed. In a mouldering city where everything was damp, she sat behind her wall of roses in absolute dryness.

"I never seem to get enough sweets for Charlie Pepper," she said and dropped an arid chunk of cake in his mouth. I watched him roll it around behind his yellow teeth, moisten it with his prickly tongue.

I tried another bite, washed it down with the tea that floated tiny flecks of leaves.

It made my eyes water, and as I blinked up again, I saw Andrew in the shadows.

He was standing silent in the doorway, head jutted forward, shoulders brooding over his hollowed chest, skeletal hands tight from shirt cuffs, limp beside the great belted stomach, massive, bloated, huge out of all proportion. His mouth was slightly open, bubbles of saliva forming on the bottom lip like a giant infant. He stared past us with eyes as still and lusterless as plastic beads.

"Oh, Andrew dear," she looked up. "Would you like your tea now? Or would you rather wait and let us have our girl talk first?"

He made a vague motion with his hand, but his eyes, his mouth didn't change. He took a step, righted himself with difficulty, his feet wobbling in blue rubber sandals. He staggered by us, listing, toes clinching the rubber thongs, on into an empty room beyond.

She smiled adoringly after him the way she always had and picked up her cup. "He had on that same color of blue shirt the first time I saw him," she said.

INCIDENT
AT FINNEGANS WAKE

THE WIND IN El Paso is omnipresent, not merely wild as the lyric says, but howling, twisting, writhing in the desert, shaping the sharp sand grit into palpable brown images that obscure the sun and cross the highway like loosened scarves. And September in the tan stone university rising out of the ash-colored cactus is drier than any Faulkner could have ever known, a month as good as any to read *Finnegans Wake* at a student-faculty colloquium.

But as I stood at the window in the dusk and watched the brown earth of the mountains sift, shift in the wind to become the air itself, I knew it was a tiresome idea, as unproductive as the desiccated blue gray of the spine-leafed century plant I could see below the edge of my balcony. I couldn't remember how I'd been urged into having it. If it were any place else I could have stayed at the Desert Hills for another drink. Granted, it'd been an adequate excuse to break away from the squat little man buying drinks for everybody in the place while he explained to me that his wife was divorcing him because he spent too much time at the track, but I could have used one more gimlet to moisten the aridity of the wind-swept afternoon, ease into the apartment weekend ahead. Perhaps I could . . . .

The doorbell rang.

The sky had darkened and the night wind hurled a brown tumbleweed past the walkway as I opened the door.

It was one of the graduate students.

"You're early."

I just stood there. I couldn't imagine any bright and eager student coming before the hour. Like a tender Yeats, they'd walk around the block for twenty minutes rather than come ahead of time.

"Am I?" He wasn't abashed. He waited in the doorway dressed in a mismatched coat and a pair of slacks no longer in style and looked as if he'd never thought of walking around the block for any reason.

I'd seen him in the halls and had nodded to him without consciously recalling his name even though I knew it was O'Neill and that he was supposed to be one of the brightest young men we had in the department.

I gestured back in the room, unable to think of an alternate greeting.

But he didn't seem to need one.

He came in and looked around and his eyes glanced off the good antiques like a quick spray. He seemed as unimpressed as he was unabashed.

"Do you want a wine?"

"Fine."

He went in the kitchen as though he knew the apartment.

His assurance irritated me. He seemed oblivious of the fact that I was the professor.

"There's some cooling," I said, but he was already at the refrigerator.

He took out the bottle and unscrewed the cap, and I had the impression that even in those wrong clothes, he was more used to wine with corks. He picked up two of the glasses I'd put out, poured them half full, and held one out to me.

I took it, but even as I did I wanted to put him in his place. "Don't you ever ask?"

He looked at me and raised his eyebrows as he screwed the lid back on the wine. He smiled. "A guy should never ask."

His eyes were as green as the bottle.

The doorbell rang again before I had to respond.

It was the stranger from the Desert Hills.

"I forgot to tell you my name a while ago when we were having drinks." He stuck out a huge plump paw with a massive turquoise ring on the middle finger. "Sam Feather. I'm a full-blooded Cherokee. I musta read every name in the El Paso phone book before I found you." He smiled disarmingly and went past me to the kitchen.

O'Neill was leaning against the sink watching us.

Just then Abel Evanston came up the walk in a lull of the wind and gave me the look of cool appraisal he wore on the occasions when we went out to dinner.

"Come in, Abel."

He touched my arm briefly with his Joycean, authoritative, distant sort of way that I interpreted as some kind of affection. I'd already heard about his break-up, not caused by the track but by the fact that his wife didn't understand the needs of academe.

We went in to where Sam Feather was drinking wine, holding the neck of a bottle protectively. He had a huge turquoise nugget set in silver on one of those bolo ties around his neck. I didn't know why I hadn't realized he was an Indian.

Then the other students arrived, almost at the same time, all on time, and a hum of vaguely uncomfortable conversation began as they got wine and groped for common topics.

Sam Feather came out of the kitchen and sat down on the Victorian plush sofa beside Abel Evanston.

I saw O'Neill standing beside the archway, a wine in his hand, his green eyes resting on me.

If there was anything I didn't need just out of my own divorce, it was to get mixed up with some twenty-two year old grad student.

I sat down on a Jacobean end table beside the couch that I didn't want anyone else to sit on. I could see that the socializing had already extended long enough. You could hear the wind at the sides of the building almost as loud as their dwindling murmurs.

I caught Abel's eye.

Since he was the Joyce man and fancied he could adopt the Irish accent necessary for the text, he'd elected to do all the reading himself. A wine bottle went around, Sam Feather gulping his glass and pouring another as it passed, Abel cleared his throat, and the room settled into listening stasis.

"Well, arundgirond in a waveney lyne aringarouma she pattered and swung and sidled, dribbling her boulder through narrowamosses, the diliskydrear on our drier side and the vilde vetchvine agin us, curara here, careero there, not knowing . . . ."

They had on their studious faces, stiff and quiet, staring hard at the floor or at the opposite wall the way people do when they listen, or appear to listen, closely, and only a few hardier souls drew sips of wine, careful to keep their gulps inaudible.

O'Neill was in the door, still looking at me.

I suddenly remembered the grafitti one of the students told me about in the second floor library men's john, "Wow!" it read, "What a semester! Three nice girls, one prostitute, and my English teacher." All I needed . . . .

". . . and raising a bit of a chir or a jary every dive she'd neb in her culdee sacco of wabbash she raabed and reach out her maundy meerschaundize, poor souvenir as per ricorder and all for sore . . . ."

Abel's voice filled the room melodiously, soothingly, and I had an almost overwhelming desire to shut my eyes. I took a mouthful of wine to keep alert, awake, and concentrated on the hard red dryness. It was with a jolt that I realized Abel had paused, not for effect, but in a profound silence, for the discussion.

The students were rigid, avoiding the first move that might draw professorial attention and a question in their direction.

"There certainly is some beautiful language in that passage," one of them finally said into the silence, showing he wasn't afraid of Joyce.

"I think the fact that Joyce worked and reworked each word for the sound, not just the meaning, is perhaps the most important aspect, don't you?" Abel said. "And there is something to having it read aloud the way Joyce suggested, of course, that you miss in merely reading the printed page."

"You're right, Dr. Evanston. It really should be read aloud," another student seconded.

It was a safe thing to say and some of the others nodded sagely, feeling easy enough to shift, unbend their cramped knees.

I glanced at Sam Feather and saw that the drinks from the Desert Hills had taken effect. He was nodding, swaying as he sat, drinking the wine like coffee.

Someone asked if they might hear a little more, murmuring that they felt we were just getting into it.

Abel turned the page and began again.

"Throw us your hudson soap for the honour of the Clane! The wee taste the water left. I'll raft it back, first thing in the marne. Merced mulde! Ay, and don't forget the reckitts . . . ," he read.

"Shuinhv lef hernkids, not furny bottlefilled, not furny thing, spacially not orsracin, not whoresracin," said Sam Feather.

A couple of the students threw shocked glances at him, but since they didn't know how to react or what to react to, they pretended they hadn't heard, and Abel raised his slipping Irish accent another pitch.

". . . potatorings boucled the loose laubes of her laudsnarers: her nude cuba stockings were salmospotspeckled: she sported a galligo shimmy of hazevaipar tinto that never was fast till it . . . ."

"Don blamer talking allen kids oaf my leif, but sad. Still don blamer tall," said Sam Feather loudly.

A flush washed up from Abel's pale neck to his eyebrows and he stopped in the middle of what was probably a sentence.

One of the more eager students said quickly, "I think Joyce has mellowed after *Ulysses*." He glanced around. "I personally find this a much more sympathetic work."

Another said as quickly, "I don't think you can say that. I think every man in Joyce's world is paralyzed by his own uninvolvement."

"Everman. Parleyed, parleyed. Feathers nothing worse, reeling whores, than drunk endyan, feathers, dunno wattis," said Sam Feather.

He was louder than the others and momentarily drowned them out. .

But then they went doggedly on, and I leaned over to him, "Don't you think it's time to go back to the motel now, Sam?"

He swivelled his head, jiggled his glass to splash purple wine on the blue silvered stone and his shirt front. "Don Juan be lone." He looked blearily from me to Abel next to him. He nudged Abel with an elbow. "Should . . . I . . . go . . . home?" he said, salivating it carefully.

Abel looked down at his thick dark face with alarm, edged away slightly. "Certainly not if you don't want to," he said hastily.

Sam Feather looked back at me and shook his head.

"No one acts now or even sees anything that requires an action," a student said.

Abel was leaning away from Sam Feather, isolating, separating himself. "I agree that we don't act, but none of us wants a man to take a stand in order to be heroic any longer. It's our idea of heroism itself that's changed."

I sat there debating how to ease him to the door, out into the parking lot and into my car. Once at the Mesa Inn where he'd said he was staying, I could lure him out of the car again with the offer of another drink.

"Our idea of heroism is that a man be gentle, understanding, a good . . . ."

How to get him up off the Victorian couch and . . . .

I glanced up and there was O'Neill beside me.

He tapped Sam Feather on the shoulder, put his other hand under his elbow and lifted him off the sofa. "Come on Sam," he said in a quiet voice. "It's time to go now."

The room looked up briefly as the two of them stood up.

"Tlate, tlaloc, niera tlaloc, tlate."

"It's not too late." He guided the swaying figure through the students and out the door.

" . . . butty don blamer . . . ." The wind caught the blurred words as the door shut.

Abel raised his voice to cover it, "You see, we simply don't need our heroes to make any kind of a gesture."

It was something they could all talk about, and as they launched into it, I got up and opened two more bottles of wine and passed them around.

The bowls of potato chips were empty except for the cigarette someone had put out in one of them.

I sat down on the end table and Abel smiled at me.

Then the door opened again and O'Neill was back. Abel was talking. "What we have today is escapism, daydreams, alienation, a sense of isolation that cuts us off from the heroes of the past."

I looked at each speaker as if I were listening and sipped the wine. It seemed a long time, but finally they began to leave.

"I'll call you for dinner next week sometime," Abel said and touched my arm.

The wind whipped against his suit coat, gusted dry leaves in tiny swirls around his feet as he hurried toward the parking lot.

I hadn't seen O'Neill leave, and as I closed the door on the last of the students murmuring politely about the stimulating evening, I saw him in the kitchen leaning against the cabinet.

Empty wine bottles, goblets, rings of red wine layered the table top.

He was looking at me and smiling.

"How old are you?" I said.

"Thirty-four. Why?"

Up close his green eyes had gold flecks in them and lines around the lids that could have belonged to someone in his thirties.

"I just wondered," I said.